29 Dimes:
A Love Story

Randolph Randy Camp

ISBN: 1492888001
ISBN 13: 9781492888000

Dedicated to my children, Natasha, Christina, Randie,
Melinda, Ranielle, and Joshua

Table of Contents

1
Silver Lake

~

Just let it out. Miss Kelley always told us that when we had to do a new project. Miss Kelley was the coolest teacher I ever had. It was a sad day when she told us that she had to leave LA and go back to Kansas to take care of her mother. I had some nasty dreams about Miss Kelley but I never did tell her though. That's actually kind of ironic 'cause she was the one who broke me out of my shell two years ago. She said to never hold back, just let it out. They call me Pepe but my real name is Peter. I hate that name Peter 'cause it's a white boy's name. Oh don't get me wrong, I ain't got nothing against white people or anything like that, but the only thing white about me is the skin I'm wearing.

It's the last day of our junior year at John Marshall High. Just like any other day, me and the crew is kicking back on lunch break at our usual spot, the center quad. I'm not supposed to be here in Silver Lake but one of my mom's work friends let me use his address so that I could come here to John Marshall. That bitch ass principal in Echo Park didn't like what I had to say about the school especially after Miss Kelley had left so they tried to silence me but that just wasn't happening. Ain't no way I'm gonna let 'em shut me down that easy. If I got something I wanna say I'm gonna say it. Period. Matter ' fact, I don't even see why they call this place Silver Lake 'cause for as long as I've been coming 'round here I ain't never seen no damn silver lake. Shit, they should've called it Silver Hills 'cause they gotta bunch of them all over the fuckin' place but I ain't never seen a silver lake. I'm sure it's around here somewhere though, probably hiding behind something else. That's what some people do here in LA..... hide. Hell, LA an' Hollywood was built on that hiding shit. I guess they figure if you can't be yourself then just throw on some makeup and turn yourself into somebody else then.

Cool, the circle is full. Everybody's here. Squatted next to me is my girl Teki. She's the one who talked me into trespassing to John Marshall when Echo Park was giving me a lot of shit about my mouth. We've been together almost a year now which is different for me 'cause normally girls dump my ass after about two weeks 'cause they can't stand my mouth either. When people ask Teki how come she's still with me she tells them that I'm like an angry, hungry puppy so she can't abandon me. Whatever.

Teki's in an all-girl Chinese reggae band. They call themselves Yello Stuff. I met Teki one night at this club down on Santa Monica. They were messing up the lyrics to one of my favorite Bob Marley songs so after they finished I walked up on stage and let Teki know how I felt about that. Teki tried her best to explain that they left out a couple of lines of the song on purpose and I felt that nobody should ever mess with Marley's words. If you don't fuck with the Bible then you shouldn't fuck with Marley's lyrics either. Anyway, Teki called me an asshole and we've been going together ever since.

Tip and Brittany are always together. Tip got that name 'cause he used to tag for the Silver Lake Boyz but he stop running with them when he started hanging with Brittany. No matter how hard he'd wash his hands, Tip always had that trademark fingertip stain from those spray cans. Ever since he's been seeing Brittany though all he does now is paint murals. Sometimes he gets paid, sometimes not. Brittany is like the black Diane Sawyer. All she ever talks about is serious shit and having her own TV news show one day. When people ask her why is she seeing somebody like Tip she says that anybody who can paint big colorful murals like that gotta have something special in him. It gotta come from somewhere she says.

Valerie hardly says anything but her beautiful face and that rocking ass body of hers is loud like a motherfucker. A lot of dudes at Marshall talk a lot of shit about being with her like guys always do but only a few actually approach her though. Some people say that Valerie is more beautiful than J-Lo and Beyonce put together. People tell her that she should be a model but a lot of them don't even know that she's a mother too. When Valerie's at school her mother keeps Valerie's little girl on the taco truck she owns 'cause they can't afford daycare or a real babysitter. Valerie's cell phone is about to blow up any minute now. It always does. It's going to be her baby's daddy. He's always bugging her but she can't turn off her phone 'cause it might be her mother calling about her daughter. Valerie's phone rings. She glances at the name on the screen and ignores it.

Kalib got brains. Kalib's a smart Armenian dude who's crazy about computers and Play Station war games. He's been trying to get with Valerie ever since I've known them. No matter how many times Valerie rejects his passes Kalib keeps coming at her harder and harder. She doesn't like it when he squats next to her 'cause he always make sure that his elbow or knee is slightly touching her, and when she scoots to break the touch he inches closer. Today's Valerie's

3

lucky day. Two Army recruiters come to her rescue. Kalib's been trying for early enlistment and all he has to do now is pass some type of psych test and then he's locked in. The recruiters give Kalib a nod. Anxiously, Kalib stands to leave. They'll take him off campus to the recruiter office up on Sunset then bring him back after the test.

"Wish me luck everybody," Kalib utters while looking at Valerie.

"Good luck, Kalib," Valerie politely says with huge relief.

Here comes Ronnie. He likes to sit with us sometimes 'cause he's another dude who's after Valerie. Ronnie's cool with me but people be making fun of him 'cause he's a little slow and in that special class. I don't know what happened to Ronnie but I figure that whatever it is it wasn't his fault. Valerie's not that hard on Ronnie like she is with Kalib, but she never had a real conversation with Ronnie at school though. So far, all Ronnie ever got from Valerie is the pity finger-wave, and that's only if he works up enough nerve to say his choppy "Hey, how ya doing?" to her. Ronnie blew my mind a couple weeks ago when he told me that he took a bus all the way out to Eagle Rock where Valerie's mom had set up their taco truck at a construction site. All Ronnie wanted was for Valerie to serve him and he was happy.

"Hey, Valerie. How ya doin'?" Ronnie nervously spits out.

As usual, Valerie is careful not to lead Ronnie on or hurt his feelings too much so she wiggles 'hello' with her fingers but hold back words that might spark a conversation. Sometimes I feel for Ronnie 'cause I know what it's like to be wanting something that you can't have. Shit, I've been feeling like that my whole life, always trying to climb out of this skin. I know Ronnie wants to know where Valerie's mom is parking their truck next but he knows it's useless for him to ask Valerie so I got his back.

"Is business good, Valerie?"

4

"Yea, Mom's got almost the whole summer at that new subdivision."

"Cool. Right here in Silver Lake?"

"Yea, you know, it's those new homes they're building up on Sanborn."

"Cool."

Ronnie's not as slow as people think he is. He knows exactly what just happened and looks at me with that silly grin of his. Now I gotta keep it going and play this shit off so Valerie won't think she got played.

"So Brittany, whatcha got going for the summer?"

"I'm so happy! I got the internship at KRCT!" Brittany beams.

"Isn't that the PBS station over there on Sunset?" Valerie asks.

"Yea, and before y'all start with the Big Bird and Sesame Street jokes they actually promised me a wrap-a-round by the end of the summer!" Brittany shines.

"Wrap a what?" Ronnie asks.

"Ronnie, it's like when you're watching the news on TV and the anchor switches it over to the reporter out on the street to do the meat of the story and then it goes back the anchor back at the desk."

Ronnie's quietly trying to absorb Brittany's explanation then blurts, "Kinda like Valerie's mom's tacos, huh?"

"Not that type of meat, Ronnie, I mean the meat, the juice of the story, oh just forget it," Brittany sighs while eying Teki for a rescue.

My man Ronnie gets that all the time. People be thinking that he doesn't get it but most of the time Ronnie sees it better than they do. It's just a different view with different eyes, that's all.

"Honestly, I'm not really looking forward to this summer. Everything's good with the band an' all and we're gigged up all summer long but I don't like it when my brother comes to LA," Teki confesses with a slight hint of Chinese.

It's kinda cool how Teki dyed half of her hair purple with strands peeping from under that yellow bandana she always wear, and I like the way her lips move when she talks too. Teki's lips are shaped just like Miss Kelley's lips. I do be listening to my girl when she's talking to me, but I gotta be real though, when Teki talks sometimes I start thinking about the special conversations me and Miss Kelley used to have after class. Miss Kelley was the first person who got me, like got me for real. Miss Kelley was older than me an' I respected her an' shit but, man, I'm tellin' ya, that lady was down wit' everything.

"I was hoping to write some original songs with the band but with Vince coming, I don't know," Teki sighs.

Nobody in the crew has ever heard Teki mention her brother before and she barely mentioned him to me. Tip is curious, "So what's up with you and your brother, Teki? Is he younger or older?"

I don't know what's the thing between my girl and her brother is all about but I can tell she don't wanna talk about him anymore by the way she does her little fake smile and looks down. I better save her, "What about you, Tip? You still working on that wall on Rowena?"

"Naw dude, that's in the bag. I put the final touches on that one on Saturday. Now I got this big ass wall near the steps. You know, that staircase where all the tourists an' joggers go. It's that grocery store about a block from there on Descanso. That'll be my biggest wall so far. That'll keep me outta trouble all summer."

I like the way Tip just lights up when he's talking about his murals. I feel like that sometimes too when I'm on stage doing my thing. Miss Kelley was right. Shit just feels good when ya getting ya shit out.

Brittany looks at me with that TV smile of hers, "So what about you, Pepe? Any special summer plans?"

"Nothing really 'cept working on some new rhymes for the street fair in a couple months."

"Yea, I know right, that's all Mom's be talking about!" Valerie jumps in, "She goes on forever an' ever about winning again at Sunset Junction!"

"Shit yea, girl. Anna's tacos is the bomb!" Tip boasts.

"For real. No doubt! Anna's the best! Mmmm, hands down!" Brittany agrees.

My man Ronnie is looking a little left out. He waves his hand as if he's in that special class asking permission to speak. I don't always rescue him 'cause sometimes you gotta let a person swim on their own. Amidst the high-fives and carrying on about Valerie's mom's tacos, Ronnie loudly stutters, "Anybody wanna know what I'm gonna be doing this summer?"

This is not the first time Ronnie has done something like this, so, on cue from Teki, in perfect unison, the whole crew turns to Ronnie and affectionately teases, "What are you doing for the summer, Ronnie?"

"Dad got this whole big batch of old dirty coins at the shop from some estate auction sale last week and he said that I had all summer to clean 'em up. Dad said that I can keep the newer ones but he's gonna resell the older ones in the shop. Y'all should see 'em! It's a lot, like really a lot! Like a whole bunch of these big jars of old sticky quarters, pennies, nickels and dimes."

Nobody says a word. Brittany and Teki want to burst out laughing but I shoot them a look. Finally, my man Tip breaks the ice, "That's cool Ronnie. That sounds real cool."

2
Sunshine

~

At first I didn't like my name Valerie, but when my mom told me how my Grandma Lucy was really the one responsible for my name then it sort of grew on me, I guess. My mom said that when Grandpa and Grandma first came to LA from Mexico they used to watch TV shows like the Mary Tyler Moore Show to learn English, and Mary was my Grandma Lucy's favorite character. Mom said that Grandma hated Mary's friend Rhoda on the show 'cause she was a bitch and was kinda mean to Mary sometimes, but when the credits rolled, Mom said that Grandma liked the actress' real name Valerie Harper though 'cause her best friend back in Mexico was named Valerie too and it always made her happy when she saw that name on the TV screen.

My Grandma Lucy and Grandpa are gone now. It's just me, Mama, and my little Sunshine Nina now. Me and my mom is kinda cool but there's one thing, kinda like this dirty shit between us that we just don't really talk about but we both know it's there, always. It all started about three years ago when I was fourteen, almost fifteen.

After waiting tables for years Mama used all of her tip savings to buy a used food truck. She couldn't afford the license fee so we only went to the few places in LA where nobody checked on that kinda stuff. We mostly parked near the big courtyard at General Hospital over in Boyle Heights. People didn't want to wait in those long lines in the cafeteria so there would be all kinds of food trucks set up outside. Mom's friend who told her about the hospital said only half of 'em was legal. People always loved my mom's tacos so that's what we sold. Since we started Anna's Taco Box, Mom never changed her prices. Most people get our Taco Special, two large tacos and a medium soda for $2.90. Competition was always pretty tight in Boyle Heights. We barely broke even most days. And then one day everything changed.

I'll never forget it. It was a Tuesday, about a half hour after the lunch rush. A construction crew was putting up a new sidewalk guard rail leading up towards the side entrance. Business was slow. Mama was making some more sauce on top of the burner off to the side of me. I was dicing onions while keeping an eye out for customers and that's when this good looking guy walked up to the window with dried cement stuck on his face. I wanted to tell him how good he looked but Mama said that good girls don't tell guys stuff like that. I was thinking a whole lot of stuff but I didn't say nothing though. I wanted to do those things with him like I'd seen those girls do to guys in them YouTube videos.

"Mama mia! You're so beautiful! I forgot what I wanted to order now. What's your name?"

"Valerie."

"Hm, Valerie. I like that. Pretty name for a pretty girl."

"Thank you. What's yours?"

"They call me Rico."

"Well, Rico, you got some cement on the right side of your face. Right there."

"Can you do me a favor Valerie and pluck it off for me? I'll step closer."

"Um, I better not 'cause —"

"Aw com'on, Valerie. I promise I won't bite ya."

"Hm...okay."

I didn't know it but Mama was listening all the time and when Rico's face got too close to mine she just shoved me aside and went all mommy dearest n' shit, "Valerie! Are you taking care of the customers? Did you finish chopping the onions?"

Mama knew from the get-go what Rico was all about so she didn't really expect me to answer her. She turned right away to Rico, "Can I take your order, please?"

After years of waiting tables, Mama took pride in knowing how to read an' deal with all kinds of people. But, for the first time, I saw my mom get played. Smooth-like, Rico gave me a wink and then he went to work on my mom, "Oh, I already gave my order to the young lady. It's six orders of your taco special for me and the guys working on the sidewalk over there. By the way, you two gotta be sisters or some'em 'cause beauty's certainly running in your family."

Mama tried to hide it but she was blushing so hard. She didn't even bother to correct him either. And on top of that, she knew that Rico didn't give me his order but none of that mattered once she heard him say six orders. Rico did a job on her. He played her good. She almost forgot why she was even mad at me. But that lasted only for about a minute until she looked at my blouse and then she was her regular self again, "Valerie, won'tcha put 'em chichi's back inside an' button that shirt all the way up like a lady. Com'on now, help me with these six specials!"

For the next two days Rico and his construction buddies was making five or six visits to our truck throughout the day. Mama made more money from Rico and his friends than all the other customers combined. Me and Mama both knew Rico was making all those trips to the truck just to see me but we didn't talk about it. I knew she didn't like it though. Mom told me about two years ago when my breasts starting growing kinda early an' guys started staring that maybe she'll let me start going out on dates probably like when I'm sixteen. Yesterday when Rico paid for his order our hands touched and he stretched his fingers out so that they would softly run along mines. I knew Mama saw it but she just turned her head slightly, pretending she didn't see anything. I guess money can make people see whatever they wanna see, or whatever they don't wanna see.

When Friday came around Rico came to the truck and asked to speak to Mom.

"Mom, it's Rico. He wants to talk to you."

While Rico was waiting for my mom to come to the window he gave me this wink like he always do but this wink was different, like he was up to something but he didn't tell me what it was though. When Mama came to the window, Rico straighten his back and pretended that he wasn't looking at my breasts. He looked so silly doing that.

Rico knew that Mom saw him staring at my tits so he was embarrassed and bowed his head a little. He tried to look her straight in the eye but couldn't pull it off. I guess he wasn't as smooth as he thought he was. I don't know why but he really looked so stupid just trying to ask my mom a simple little question.

"Anna, you gotta moment?"

I could tell by the way Mom looked at Rico and then shifted her eyes at me that she thought Rico was going to ask her something about me.

"Rico, my daughter's only fourteen and –"

"No, no, Anna, this ain't nothing like that. I just wanted to let you know that today's our last day here at the hospital. We'll be done with the rail this evening but we gotta big job at Figueroa and Third, and we're definitely gonna be there for awhile. I already got the okay from the big boss if you wanna come out every day. Here's our card with that Figueroa address on the back."

From that moment on, Rico and Mom had this kinda weird understanding between them, like quiet business partners or some shit like that. They didn't sign any papers or do a handshake but an agreement was made between those two that day. I didn't realize it then but it was that very agreement that I paid for later.

❊❂❊

For the next two years business was a whole lot better. Mama would follow Rico and his construction buddies to all of their jobs around LA plus we got good word-of-mouth too. People started talking about my mom's tacos like they would drive way across LA just to get 'em. Business was so good that, for the first time, Mom started throwing a few dollars my way after she paid all the bills. She finally got legit too. Mama was so happy when she got that permit. She even took pictures with it. She was like all crying an' shit. She said that it would've been real sweet if Grandpa and Grandma Lucy was still here to see it.

Every day when we would be at the construction site Rico would wait until Mom left to go to the bank and I would be alone.

At first I only let him suck my nipples but then he started begging for more. One day he got me all wet and I lost control. About two months after that I started getting sick a lot so I went to the Free Clinic up on the boulevard. I didn't want Mom knowing where I was going so that's why I went there. This girl had told me that I didn't need my mom to sign anything if I went there. I told my mom I was going to be back at the site in a few hours. After I got the news from the clinic that day I didn't know what to think or do. Getting pregnant wasn't something I planned on or even knew anything about. All I knew was that it was something Mama always warned me about. After this real nice lady at the clinic schooled me on a few things and walked me through the whole process, I kinda felt okay and she even set me up with all that prenatal care stuff too. She was like so cool. When I was heading back to the construction site I was a little nervous 'cause I knew I had to tell my mom but I wasn't sure how or when I should tell Rico. As I got closer to our truck I noticed the side flap was pulled down to cover the customer window, like we do when we're closed or something, so I walked around the back and pulled open the rear door. The stuff I seen that day taught me more about men than any textbook or YouTube video could ever teach me. And people always say to me, "Valerie, why are you so quiet now?" For real yo, they just don't know. When I opened that back door they didn't even see or hear me at first. When the door slammed behind me, Rico came rushing out trying to explain, but he looked so stupid like he always do, trying to say something that's really simple and so obvious, which is the fact that he's just a no good dog.

※❂※

When I had Nina I started calling her my little Sunshine right away 'cause she was the only bright thing in my life. I can't wait 'til this summer is over 'cause things gonna be so sweet once I get that last year of school over with and I can spend more time with my little Sunshine.

3
The Lesson

~

"Peter! Hey Peter!"

Man, Kalib's all brainy an' techy an' shit but he's a stubborn dude. I keep telling him to call me Pepe but he still calls me Peter with that thick Armenian accent that sounds more like Russian to me. The recruiters dropped Kalib off just before fifth period. The hallway was filled with that last-day-of-school fuse and every student was getting ready to explode at 2:45 sharp.

"Peter, wait up! Peter!" Kalib stretched his head above the crowd to get my attention. He didn't know I'd already spotted him. How can you not notice him? Kalib's about the most tensed dude I know. My girl Teki don't like Kalib 'cause she don't like the way he keep coming at Valerie. I went over his house a few times 'cause we used to play NBA 2K and Madden NFL but then he got real obsessed with those war games like Kill I, Kill II, and shit like that. After Kalib got deep into those war games I stop going to his house but we're still cool though. Teki thinks Kalib only uses people to try an' get at Valerie but I don't care if that's true or not 'cause like I always say, I know what it's like to be wanting something you can't have.

Everybody's scattering to their last class of the day. The tardy bell's going to ring in about ten seconds so whatever Kalib has to tell me he better say it quick.

"Peter, wait for me after school! I gotta ask you something!"

"No problem, but can you call me Pepe next time, dude?

※❂※

I know people be thinking that I'm slouching off of Teki 'cause she be pulling down pretty money with the band but I got my own game. They don't know it but I'm still peeling off cash from that grand prize at the Venice Spoken Word Jam last summer. Every now and then, especially on these hot LA days we got now, I like to treat Teki out at Paula's Ice Cream Parlor up on Los Feliz. That's where we're hanging out later this evening, and I'd invited Kalib to meet us there 'cause he had something important to tell me, ask me, or some shit. Teki don't really care for Kalib but she never tries to control me like that. She says it's better for me to be on a long leash than a short one. Whatever.

Lately, you never know what's up with Kalib. When I used to hang with him at his house, Kalib told me that his mom got real mad one day and took down every picture on the walls of his father 'cause she didn't want to see his face anymore, and by accident, she threw away one of Kalib's framed school pictures 'cause he and his dad looked so much alike. And Kalib said that when his mom tried to apologize to him after she'd realized what she'd done, all he could do is walk away.

Yeah, I know. I could've taken Teki to Baskins Robbins or any other ice cream joint in Echo Park or Silver Lake but I like to splurge on Teki to let her know I appreciate her. That's why I brought her to

Paula's. It's weird how only a few blocks can make a person feel like a millionaire. Some people in LA come to Los Feliz to shed their skin but we only came here this evening for Paula's rocking ass banana splits. There're nine bucks and worth every single dime.

I blurt out a lot of shit and I don't even give a fuck what people think but some things about Miss Kelley I keep under wraps 'cause I don't wanna hurt Teki. About a week before Miss Kelley left LA I had this dream that me and her was walking together on the Santa Monica pier eating those big waffle ice cream cones the vendors sell there. I try not to think about Miss Kelley when Teki's lips wrap around the little mixture of ice cream, banana, fudge, and whip topping on her spoon but, man, it's hard! I wish Kalib would hurry up and get here already to save my ass. Where is he? He said it was some'em important so I know he's coming. Hurry up, Kalib! Fuck!

"Hey Peter. Hi Teki."

I never been so glad to see Kalib like right now. Sometimes I have a real hard time shaking these thoughts of Miss Kelley.

"I forget that's your real name," Teki giggles.

"See, Kalib. Dude, you gotta stop calling me Peter."

"Man, look at the size of 'em splits! They look like carnival ships!"

"Yea, man, Paula don't play. She ain't skimpy on nothing. I like it like that. Everybody should be like Paula. Here, I got you, dude. Take this ten spot and come back an' we'll talk business."

"You're the man, um…Pepe."

"See, there ya go."

She's trying to be cool as possible but I see Teki giving me the eye.

"I appreciate you coming Teki. When I told Kalib that you would be with me he said that he didn't mind."

I could tell that Teki wanted to snatch my head off by the way her eyes shifted and almost closed but she didn't say a word though. See, that's what I like about Teki. She got class. 'Em girls I used to hang out with would've had Paula's best all over my face by now. But not Teki. She wrapped 'em Miss Kelley lips of hers around another scoop of Paula's tasty split and let it slide down her throat like she wasn't even thinking about me or Kalib. Man, was I wrong. The second Kalib came back to the table and sat down right across from Teki she shot me a look I'd never seen before and it scared the shit out of me! I didn't know what to do but I knew enough not to say anything to Teki right now.

"So, how'd you think you did on that Army psych test, Kalib?"

"They said they'll let me know in about three days. I think I nailed it though."

For some reason Kalib kept glancing at my girl's hair. He had this look like he wanted to ask her something but I didn't get a chance to warn him not to.

"Teki, can I ask you some'em? Did your parents mind it when you colored your hair purple? I never saw an Asian girl with purple hair before. Normally, Chinese people are very strict about their culture. Or maybe you probably did it for the band, huh?"

I knew Teki wasn't going to answer Kalib. Instead, she gave me one of her looks. But I didn't need her look to tell me I better change the subject. I was already on it.

"So what's up, Kalib? You wanna tell me some'em? What's on ya mind, dude?"

"Teki, I'm sorry if I said something wrong about your hair or —"

"Forget about my hair, Kalib. You want me to leave so you can feel more comfortable talking to Pepe alone?"

"No, no. Don't leave. I'm glad you're here, Teki. It's better that both of —"

"Dude! Com'on now, what's up?"

"Alright. Here it is. I want to try one more time with Valerie an' I was hoping since you guys are closer to her than me that maybe you can talk to her for me. I really like her. I really do! She's not like other girls. Valerie's quiet and nice."

I wish my man Kalib would've never had said that. That's the first time I saw Teki's face turn red! I could feel the heat coming from her skin.

"What exactly do you mean by 'like other girls', Kalib? Are you talking about girls like me, Kalib?"

"No, I didn't mean it like that. I'm just nervous, that's all. You see, I've been thinking about this for a long time. It's like a plan."

I don't know if it was the word 'plan' or just the way it came out of Kalib's mouth but it got stuck in my girl's ear and she couldn't get it out.

"A plan? What kinda plan, Kalib?"

"I was thinking that maybe Valerie could come over and we could talk an' play this new really cool game I just got called 'Call Signal One'! See, it's about these snipers see! They're the good guys an' they have to spot and take out the terrorist trying to blend in this big huge crowd with a cell ph—"

"Wait! So you want me and Pepe to ask Valerie, a girl who you're trying to impress, to go to your house to play a game that kills people?"

"Um…why you have to say it like that? The snipers are the good guys and —"

"And what? A nice quiet girl like Valerie would love her first date with you and seeing blood splatter from the heads of people standing in a crowd with cell phones?"

"Why you have to put it like that, Teki?"

"I'm sorry, Kalib, but I can't help you."

Not a second went by and Kalib had his serious eyes on me, only this time they were almost crying to me like I was the only person in this world who could help him. I was too afraid to look at Teki but I could feel her eyes on me too, only her eyes were kinda burning my skin again.

"I tell ya what, Kalib —"

"Pepe, if you wanna help Kalib then help him but don't expect me to say one single word to Valerie. I'm out, okay?"

Me and Kalib glance at one another without words. He gave me a nod like dudes do, and then he tried to hide a tiny smile 'cause he knew I had his back, but my girl Teki didn't like this shit at all.

❊❊❊

Kalib went home happy with the hope that I might set him up with Valerie over the summer. It's sad to say it but the hard truth is that Kalib's happiness lasted about seventeen minutes, that's how long it takes to walk from Paula's Ice Cream Parlor in Los Feliz to his mother's house in Silver Lake. Kalib told me that after his mother had mistakenly taken his picture off the wall he no longer felt like their house was his home too. Unlike me, Kalib had a taste of his father, but now his mother is trying to wash all memories of him away. I'm not a history buff and I barely got a 'C' in Global Studies but from the shit Kalib's been schooling me on and the stuff I'd seen with my own eyes when I used to go to his house to play Madden NFL, that terrible shit that went down about a hundred years ago between Turkey and Kalib's people is still fucking up his family today. Kalib says his mother tries to forgive and forget how the Turks killed over two million Armenians but his father has trouble trying to shake those memories and he carries around bitterness and hatred that leaks out after a few beers.

I realize I pissed off my girl Teki this evening, but I know too much about Kalib's routine and I just couldn't say no to him.

The moment Kalib turns the doorknob to walk in, his mother, Adelina, will be standing there and she's going to start off barking at him with reminders about how much his cell phone and games cost an' then she's gonna bitch at him for leaving the Play Station power on and Kalib's going straight to his room without him ever mentioning a single word about the Army recruiters, his psych test, or his summer hopes with Valerie. That's just how it is at 192 Prospect Avenue.

❈❈

At 3780 Silver Lake Boulevard, Mr. Ronald Abelson and his wife Amy are tending to a handful of avid hobbyist and collectors as they have been for the past twenty-two years. Vibrant gold and blue letters on the window pane proudly boasts...

SILVER LAKE COINS & STAMPS
WE BUY & SELL RARE & COLLECTIBLES
VINTAGE U.S. STAMPS
SILVER & GOLD COINS
CALL (323) 444-4360

In the back room, a small radio fills the air with a catchy tune that Ronnie hums along to and inserts the name 'Valerie' where the girl's name 'Cherry' supposed to be. Ronnie sits with a large tub of soapy solution between his legs. Behind him is a bank of shelves

23

lined with large jars of greasy, gum-stuck, candy-stained old coins that Ronnie's dad finds at big estate auctions on the weekends. A cafeteria-size table draped with thick drying towels is fixated just to the left of Ronnie as he flips and twirls his gloved hands into the sudsy liquid, gently rubbing the dirty coins as they slip and sink between his fingers.

Stupid Sandy Molsen. I don't know why they put me in the slow class but they did get it right when they put stupid Sandy in there though. All she do is complain and complain. She don't like Silver Lake 'cause she says it got too many hills an' she gotta climb a thousand steps up to her house, but I like Silver Lake though. I like Silver Lake 'cause Valerie lives in Silver Lake.

"How's it going back here, Junior? I heard you back here humming an' singing. Remind me never to take you to the American Idol auditions, alright?"

"Ha ha, very funny, Dad."

"So what's on your mind lately, Junior? Anything new?"

"Dad, can I ask you some'em?"

"Anything. You know that."

"Dad, how do you get a girl to talk to you?"

"Hold on a sec, let me grab another chair from the closet. So who's the girl?"

"Her name's Valerie. She's beautiful, Dad. But she won't even talk to me."

"Junior, when me an' your mom were kids we lived over on Ivy Hill an' after school the bus used to let us off at the bottom so every day we had to climb these steps, so every day I would ask Amy if she wanted me to carry her up the steps and —"

"Dad, you couldn't carry —"

"I knew that and your mom knew that but she just smiled and kinda giggled every time I'd asked, and that's my point, Ronnie."

"Dad, I don't think Valerie and her mom lives on a hill and —"

"No, no, no. You're missing my point. Ronnie, from this day forward, whoever this Valerie is, I want you to approach her with something really special and different. Just think of something that will make her remember you. Just be consistent, and trust me, she'll never forget you. Even if she don't respond to you at first, eventually she will because you'll be in her mind even when you're not around."

"Hmm."

"Hey, I gotta make a run to get a bite to eat for me and your mom. You want some'em?"

"Naw, I'm gonna take a walk and get a taco special when I take my break later on."

"Wow, just look at how shiny you're getting those dimes! Now remember, Junior, you go ahead an' keep the newer coins that I can't sell out front."

4
Teki

~

"Arghhhhh, Teki! Ughhhh!"

My parents would get so frustrated with me because I never did fit squarely into their expectations of the typical 'Chinese girl' box. I was always spilling out around the edges. For some reason, music came naturally to me but I didn't care for the structural movements of Bach, Mozart and Beethoven. After spending a ton of money for my classical piano lessons at the Gifted Prodigy Academy I blew their minds at my first and last recital when I played a reggae version of Mozart's 'Allegro'.

"Arghhhhh, Teki! Ughhhh!"

To my parents, I'm different. But to me, I'm just being me an' that's what I like about my boyfriend too. Some people sees him like a white boy trying to be black or Hispanic or whatever but Pepe's just being Pepe. On the surface, I know my parents don't like a lot of stuff I do or who I choose to hang out with, but about three months ago me and my dad had a long talk an' told me that deep down he had a lot of respect for me and Pepe 'cause it takes a lot of courage to do the stuff we're doing and go against the grain.

Dad reminded me how hard it was for him bringing the family business from Vancouver to LA in the early days. Still today some of the students from school and jealous neighbors in Silver Lake sometimes tease and taunt us about making dirty money from the LA pimps, hookers and lowlife drug peddlers who frequent our hotels and motels scattered across the city. One of our neighbors even wrote a letter to the mayor complaining that a family involved in the Chinese Mafia and making a good living from the slimy LA underworld shouldn't be living comfortably next door to them in Silver Lake. My dad's a smart businessman and he said that if I ever felt obligated to respond to any of the teasing at school just tell them that all of his motels and hotels are above ground and all of his paperwork is legit.

I don't get involved with the family business. After school and especially during the summer I'm super busy with rehearsals and planning gigs for Yello Stuff but my brother Vince calls every summer his playtime. During the spring and fall, Vince works on his masters in business economics in Vancouver. Ever since he convinced Dad five years ago that, if he gave him one hundred dollars on Monday he could turn it into one thousand bucks by Friday evening, my dad has had Vince come to LA every summer to help out with the family business. I love my brother but we come from two different schools. I was educated on Marley's positive vibe but my brother got schooled by the mighty dollar and all the ways to divide and multiply it, clean or otherwise.

Mom picked up Vince at LAX yesterday. He's only been here one day an' already I'm getting that queasy feeling. He called me early this morning asking me to bring my guitar and meet him at our Los Feliz Manor later today. I love my brother but I'm not looking forward to this.

✖✖

About a year ago, two thousand miles away in Kansas, a job interview took place at the Mayville County school district office…

Miss Kelley has the kind of face that all boys dream about. Her hair is tossed around as if she doesn't care. Planted behind his glossy, oak desk ornamented with family photos and fancy paper weights, Deputy Superintendent Mark Clearfield scans over Miss Kelley's application and resume with a peculiar grin. A bit weary, Miss Kelley drove thirty miles from Kansas City this morning and she's anxious to hear the verdict.

"Miss Kelley, I've been working around kids practically all of my adult life and if I've learned anything from them little rug rats it's spotting bullshit and when I read on your application that you came back to Kansas to take care of your mother, well, I just had to find out –"

"But can I –"

"Listen, Miss Kelley, I spoke to Principal Thornton at Echo Park High and he explained everything about you and some kid named Pepe or Peter spending a lot of questionable time together and –"

"But I can –"

"Don't worry, Miss Kelley, I got all I needed to know and –"

"But I can –"

"Miss Kelley, Mayville got some embarrassing ass dropout numbers and we could use some fresh eyes and fresh ideas to help turn things around. I've been doing this a long time and I love those kids. I don't give a rat's ass how much time you spend with your students. If it's not showing up on the six o'clock news and your kids are getting A's and B's then I'm happy."

"I got the job?"

"Welcome to Mayville, Miss Kelley. We got the new teacher orientation coming up in a couple weeks. I'll shoot you an email."

"I got the job! Yes!"

"By the way, Miss Kelley, Principal Thornton told me to tell you that although you guys had some harsh words he wanted you to know that he honestly respects you for leaving quietly and preventing that kid Peter or whatever you guys called him from getting mixed up in a school board investigation."

"Hm, it's so easy for him to say that now but Thornton knows that he was flat out wrong. I'm a great teacher. I try to be straight forward and totally upfront with my kids 'cause that's how you connect with them. If a student and I talked privately to get a better connection I see no problem with that. I love being a teacher and my goal is to get the most out of each and every one of my students. I love it when they release their inhibitions and just let things out. To me, that's what teaching is all about."

"Miss Kelley, I have no doubt about where your heart's at, but you can tell me about one thing though, your mother. How's she doing?"

"Oh, she's prepping for the Kansas City marathon next month. She's up to some'em like three miles per day now and determined to beat her finish time last year."

"Aha, I kinda figured that. Where'd you get that 'I gotta go back to Kansas because my mom's sick' line anyway? That's worst than 'my dog ate my homework'."

※❂※

Back in Silver Lake, today's the day Pepe makes good on his promise to Kalib. He's walking up the hill on Sanborn, on his way to talk to Valerie. With every step Pepe makes, he sees Tip's past as a tagger on every visible wall and street pole. Animated graffiti style letters spelling out 'SILVER LAKE BOYZ' and sometimes the abbreviated 'SLB' flash out at every angle. But what really catch the eye are the colorful talents of Tip's new creations. Two blocks from the new subdivision under construction, the left wall of Susie's Flower Shop is graced with an explosion of vibrant colors on a mural depicting an angelic, beautiful woman with long flowing hair reaching down through the white, puffy clouds handing long stem purple roses to a group of children looking up at the crystal blue sky.

Nearing the construction site, Pepe hastily grab at words as he rehearses his lines...

"Hey now Valerie, you should give Kalib a chance. Nah, too bland. What's up Valerie, did I tell ya' how much Kalib likes you? That's stupid. She already knows that. What's up Valerie, you and Kalib should go out. Argghhhh. Man, this shit's hard. Valerie, I'm not cupid but you and Kalib would make a cool couple. Argghhhhhh. Hey look Valerie, I'm gonna be for real with you. I know Kalib can seem a little rude sometimes but he just needs a friend. We gotta winner."

Pepe reach a graveled cutaway lined with the construction workers' beefy trucks and SUV's. Casually strolling by a red Ford F-250 pickup, Pepe suddenly freeze as his eyes lock in on Anna's Taco Box parked near two large eucalyptus trees in the corner of the bustling site. What stopped Pepe dead in his tracks wasn't the mere site of the lunch truck, but rather the site of the dude walking towards it. Seeing his buddy Ronnie stepping closer to the customer window puts a triumphant grin on Pepe's face.

"Go 'head, Ronnie. Make that move," Pepe quietly cheers.

The eucalyptus trees throw plenty of shade across the front of the lunch truck but Pepe has no doubt about the dude standing at the window digging deep into his pants pocket with his right hand. With his mission and promise to Kalib briefly side-tracked, Pepe keeps his eyes on Ronnie as if he's watching the final seconds of a football game, hoping for a game-winning score. Valerie's daughter Sunshine is playing with Barbie dolls and colorful jewelry accessories at one of the two picnic tables the carpenters had made and set up under the leafy trees.

As always, a poster size sign advertizes Anna's best seller…
TACO SPECIAL $2.90
2 TACOS plus 1 MEDIUM SODA

On the other side of the service window, Anna sorts and counts the money in the cash register while Valerie lines up taco shells on a sheet pan. Bowls of fresh lettuce and tomatoes are on the prep counter next to Valerie. Anna notices Ronnie quietly standing at the window with his right hand oddly balled. Anna turns to her daughter then sighs, "Val, you better take the window now. It's that boy who only wants you to serve him."

"Mom, I can't. I haven't chopped the rest of the lettuce and tomatoes yet."

"Alright, but you know how he is," Anna sighs again.

"Hi, can I take your order?"

"Um…um, can Valerie do it?"

"Val! Get over here — told ya!"

"Argghhh — okay."

"Um, how ya doing, Valerie?"

"Can I take your order?"

"Thank you Valerie for coming to the windo —"

"May I take your order, please?"

Anna is trying her best to contain the laugh itching to burst out but can't seem to hide her cracking smile as her daughter pretends not to know Ronnie's order, an order he hasn't changed in nearly a year and a half.

"Um, yeah. I like the taco special."

"That'll be two-ninety."

Ronnie's been dreaming about this moment all night long. Wearing a mile-wide grin, Ronnie raises his balled right fist then slowly opens his fingers, unleashing twenty-nine spotless sparkling dimes upon the counter. And just as Ronnie had dreamt, Valerie's eyes widen in awe at the small mound of glistening coins.

"Oh, Mom, look! Come here — look! They shine like diamonds!"

Ronnie's face beams as Valerie and her mom are momentarily mesmerized by the radiant coins. Heeding his father's advice, from now on, Ronnie will return everyday to buy his taco special with twenty-nine shimmering dimes until Valerie is thinking of him even when he's not around.

"Maybe our neighbor on Rowena, you know, Mary's boyfriend Manny, can make a necklace or bracelet out of 'em. He's the one who makes jewelry out of anything an' sells it at swap meets and at the street fair every year," Anna suggests.

Meanwhile, watching from a distance, Pepe realizes that there's no way he can break the street code among dudes and interrupt Ronnie's move on Valerie with a pep talk to her about Kalib. Pepe quietly slips away, unseen.

Reneging on his promise to Kalib is eating at Pepe. On his walk back down Sanborn, he tries to figure a way out of the hole he'd gotten himself into. He practices several lines, "See, Kalib, what happened was I went there and then — nah. Yo, Kalib, dude, hey look — nah. Yo, Kalib, dude, look man, I — aargghhh. Man, I'm fucked. Shit!"

Nearing the bottom of Sanborn, one of Tip's vivid murals gracing the side of Carlos' Auto Repair, is a welcomed distraction for Pepe. Tip's thirty-foot masterpiece shows two kids blowing giant, crystal blue bubbles as they poke their heads out the window of a lime-green '79 low-rider Monte Carlo accented with sparkling silver rims. Inside some of the floating bubbles a mini-yellow sun radiates with shooting golden rays while other bubbles burst open with a shower of tiny crystal blue teardrops.

❈❈

Back up the hill at the construction site, sitting at the picnic table underneath the eucalyptus trees, Ronnie is enjoying his taco special as Valerie's inquisitive little Sunshine joins him and entertains him with her Barbie dolls and a few questions.

"Grandma says you like my mom. Is that true?"

"Uh huh"

"I like her too. What's your name?"

"Ronald Abelson, Junior. But most people just call me Ronnie."

"My real name is Nina but Mommy calls me Sunshine. But sometimes though, she calls me motor mouth."

"Sunshine! Don't bother the customers!" Valerie yells.

The sound of Valerie's voice steals Ronnie's attention. While watching Sunshine, Valerie's eyes catch Ronnie's gaze. Their eyes briefly lock. A weird tinkling feeling invades Ronnie's body. He's never experienced such a feeling before. He's unsure of what to do. He breaks eye contact with Valerie then awkwardly turns his head away. Valerie smiles at Ronnie's innocence then ponders the what if and the maybe.

5
Los Feliz

~

A yellow taxi pulls into the half-circle driveway of the Los Feliz Manor then stops curbside. Looking like a Hollywood starlet, disguised behind dark shades and a droopy, wide-brim hat, Teki steps out of the back seat with her guitar case in tow.

Sitting comfortably in the lobby lounge sipping on a large mai tai, Teki's brother Vince, smartly draped in a tailored blazer and sharp Stacy Adams alligators, glances at his fancy sports watch that says 'yea, I got money.'

Without looking around, Teki steps into the lobby and heads straight toward the bar and lounge area. She knows exactly where to find her brother. Vince places his mai tai aside then stands as Teki nears the row of thick-cushion leather chairs underneath an elegant, dimly lit chandelier. Teki gently rests her guitar case in one of the plush chairs then greets her brother with a sisterly kiss on the cheek….and then a quick, swift stomp of her right foot on Vince's left foot!

"Ooouucchh! What was that for?"

"That was for last summer."

"That's a long time to hold a grudge. You ever considered taking anger management classes, Teki?" Vince quips with a teasing grin.

Removing her Hollywood shades and droopy hat, Teki sinks into a leather chair. Vince shoots her twisted look, "Why are you hiding?"

"After last summer? How can you even ask me that? And why did you want me to bring my guitar?"

Coolly, Vince ignores the question as he takes a seat and reach for his mai tai resting atop a nearby end table.

"Sis, you want something to drink from the bar?"

"No, I prefer to be sober when I'm dealing with you."

"Ouch! ....I'm serious, you should really look into that anger management thing."

"Oh, cut the crap Vince an' just tell me what great business venture you're up to now."

"I kinda got myself into a lit'l jam. I promised a client a girl who could sing and play the guitar then here I am looking stupid 'cause not one single one of my um, my contacts kno —"

"Contacts? Is that what you're calling your bitches now?"

"Anyway, none of my contacts knows how to play the guitar or carry a tune."

"Who's the client?"

"Peluche."

"Isn't that French? I remember that word from linguistics class. I think it means skin or flesh."

"Well, it's not his real name. That's just what he calls himself. Teki, I don't need to tell ya this stuff, but this is Los Angeles. This is where people come to play. People here change their names all the time. Names are just like make up here. They put it on — they take it off."

"Is that it? You need a female singer?"

"Um, well, kinda sort of. You see, this guy's a naturalist."

"And?"

"Well, he's a nudist and he loves music just as much as you do, Teki."

"So what?"

"See, here's the thing, whenever he's listening to music he wants to see it and hear it naturally, if you get my drift."

"Naturally?… Where do you meet these people?"

"Um, yea…he told me that even when he's watching a music video he envisions the singer in the nude."

"So Dad spends tons of money on your college economics major and you learn how to pimp your lit'l sister?"

"Aw, look who's talking smack, the child prodigy who turns a Beethoven recital into a slamming reggae party. And I don't need to remind you how I kept your lit'l secret rendezvous from Dad."

"So now you're trying to pull a guilt trip on me? That was like four years ago. I was still in Vancouver then."

"Do you really think it matters to your Chinese dad that his thirteen year old Chinese daughter was in LA or Vancouver if he knew she was sneaking out to some reggae concert with a Black guy?"

"He was the bass player in the –"

"Okay then, just tell Dad that. Look, sis', I –"

"No, you look, Vince. Dad's not like that. He's not as shallow as you. I found that out after moving here."

"Alright, I don't wanna argue about family stuff. I want you to walk outta here with eight hundred bucks in your pocket. I know how you like to carry your weight and pay for your band's studio rehearsal time without asking Dad for a dime, so if you're willing to help your brother then –"

"Aaargghhh!"

"I'll take that as a 'yes'….And, hey sis', you know I wouldn't put you in a dangerous spot –"

"Yeah, right…..I'm kidding. I know you wouldn't, Vince. But I'm not taking everything off."

"Not to be so blunt, but I think nipples is kinda his thing… Can't you hide 'em behind the guitar when you're playing?"

"Aarggghhh!"

"I'll take that as another 'yes'. By the way, he's up on the third floor in room 312."

Coolly, Vince slips his hand into his blazer pocket to retrieve a stuffed envelope. He softly places the envelope into his sister's lap.

"Can't believe we have the same mother," Teki sighs.

※※

Carrying her guitar case, Teki steps off of the third floor elevator. She takes a few steps down the hall then taps lightly on door 312.

"It's open."

Teki slowly enters the darken room with a thin beam of sunlight sneaking through a crack in the drawn curtains. Sitting on the edge of the bed shamelessly naked is a middle-age man with graying hair. An empty desk chair is positioned a few feet directly in front of him.

"My my, well, hello there. Vince promised me a looker and he certainly kept his promise. You can sit right here in this chair where I can clearly hear and see what mother nature gave you."

Fully dressed, Teki calmly plants herself in the chair then casually finger-brush her long strands of purple hair from her face.

"Hm, I'm not one for hair dyes but I must admit that purple fits you very well, young lady."

Teki nods 'thank you' while opening her guitar case.

"I can tell by your Martin guitar that music means a lot to you. Not everybody can afford a Martin."

"Yeah, I play in a reggae band. All girls."

"All girls? Heavenly, pure heaven. And a reggae band on top of that. There's nothing more soothing than a cool reggae rhythm, especially roots reggae…I love it."

"Would you like to hear something new I've been working on? I'm still working on the melody an' the lyrics still needs a lit'l tweaking though…Wanna hear it?"

"Sure, but um…did the fellow Vince explain that —"

"Oh, that's right…I forgot."

Teki peels off her blouse then swallows her tongue as her loosen bra reveals her perky brown nipples.

"Yes, indeed, that Vince fellow sure sent me a diamond. Wow, mother nature sure is wonderful. Have you been working for Vince long?"

"No, just met him not too long ago."

"I tell ya what, that Vince has an extremely good business mind for someone his age. He's like the perfect Wall Street type but he needs to loosen up a bit though. He's wound up too tight for such a young man."

"Trust me, I'll gladly let him know that," Teki says while slyly raising her guitar to cover her puffy breasts.

"Darling, will you be a sweetheart and lower that beautiful Martin just a tab, please?"

Reluctantly, Teki lowers her six-string then begins to strum a smooth, rock-steady rhythm to escape into the world in which she's been running to ever since she was a little girl.

"I like it, I like it!…Whatcha call it?"

"Vehicles. It's about people using one another only to get to wherever they're going then just dropping them."

"I love that beat. You're very gifted. Com'on, let me hear that your voice of yours."

Strumming a melodic reggae rhythm, Teki sings in soft sweet voice....

"You pick me up....take me around
You use me up when you're feelin' down
Just like vehicles goin' around and around
Just like vehicles in my town
You only need me when you're down
Next time when you're passin' by
I'll remember you....and the smile and the lie
'Cause you're just another vehicle goin' by and by
Yeah, just another vehicle goin' by and by"

The swaying of Teki's plump breasts to the smooth rhythm of her six-string has gotten Peluche worked up seconds from an exploding wet dream. His eyes begin to roll back into his head as his right hand hastily strokes his throbbing shaft.

Oblivious to what's happening on the bed mere feet in front of her and wrapped in her own blissful world, Teki slows the rhythm and brings her song to a close...

"You hold me
You kiss me
You give me a ride
Maybe some day
Maybe some way
We may collide."

※❈※

Pepe is making his way to 192 Prospect Avenue. The quiet street of modest, single story homes is lined with lofty California palms. Toting a full sack, a mailman crosses the street several yards ahead. Kalib's mother Adelina is on her knees weeding her bountiful flowerbed as Pepe enters the yard.

"Hey, Miss Takesian, is Kalib home?"

"Hello, Pepe. I'm not old yet. Call me Adelina, I told you.... What's wrong? You don't have your smile today."

The mailman approaches and hands Adelina several pieces of mail, "You got the most colorful flowers on Prospect, Adelina."

"Thank you...... See, Pepe, everybody calls me Adelina."

Adelina quickly scans and sift through the handful of envelopes then suddenly stop and stares at one particular piece.

"United States Army? Hm, Pepe, you know anything about this?"

Smartly, Pepe shakes his head 'no.'

"Here, take it to Kalib. He's in there playing those stupid games."

Thinking that the Army recruiters' letter would bring better news to Kalib than his, Pepe gladly takes the envelope from Adelina and makes his way into the house.

※❈※

Comfortably nestled into the sofa oddly postioned next to his bed, Kalib is enthralled in an intensed moment of 'Call Signal One' playing on the 52 inch TV screen mounted on the wall. On the screen, hundreds of casually dressed pedestrians are walking along the city sidewalks. Kalib's eyes are rapidly scanning the busy crowd, trying to spot terrorists disguised as pedestrians using their cell phones. With a tight grip on the remote control, his fingers are at the ready for a quick takedown.

The loud, pulsating soundtrack of Kalib's game is drowning out Pepe's knocks on Kalib's bedroom door. Holding the envelope in his left hand, Pepe turns the knob and steps in.

Pepe steps in front of Kalib to get his attention.

"Peter!"

Kalib lowers the volume then gesture Pepe to take a seat.

"Dude, are you ever gonna call me Pepe?"

"Hey, did you talk to Valerie yet? What she say?"

"Oh, before I forget, your mom gave me this letter to give to you."

Excitedly, Kalib rips the envelope and opens the letter. Silently reading the opening lines, Kalib's face and shoulders seem to shrink as if he was taking his last breath.

"Kalib? Kalib?"

Kalib is stunned by the disappointing news. He stares at the soundless screen without the slightest motion as Pepe tries to reach him.

"Kalib?....Hey, you don't need the Army anyway. You're a smart dude who can get a computer job anywhere you want. Shit man, computer savvy dudes like you are in big demand. You don't need the fucking Army, dude."

Kalib calmly sighs, but Pepe easily reads the anger slowly festering in Kalib's twisting face as he slowly unleashes his buried thoughts, "How can they expect us just to forget it like it never happened? Dad used to tell me about how my great grandfather was killed for no reason by the Turks. For no fucking reason! Peter, this thing is like a cancer, worst than a cancer. It keeps spreading an' killing, even killing all of us who think we're free an' safe in America now – they killed us too! When the Turks killed my people back then they killed all us too, Peter!"

Concerned, Pepe puts his hand on Kalib's shoulder, "It's okay, Kalib. You made it this far, you'll get through this, dude."

Kalib shakes off Pepe's hand then erupts, tossing the remote at the wall, "Fuck it! I don't care anymore! I tried so hard Peter! I can't even get a girl here! And now the army says I'm fucking crazy! It's like the more I keep tryin' to be here the more people keep treating me like I don't belong here! Peter, I swear, all I ever tried to do is give my mom an' dad some new memories here in America, make them proud of their son! And now I can't even pass a simple psych test! Nobody fuckin' care! I don't give a shit anymore!"

Adelina burst into the room! "Kalib! Kalib, what's going on in here?"

Unable to contain his burning thoughts, Kalib frantically cries out, "Everybody remembers the Jews' holocaust but they forgot about us! Nobody talks about the Armenian genocide! Fuckin' nobody!"

"Oh, shut up Kalib! You're talking crazy just like your father! Maybe if you got outta this awful smelly room an' go out an' meet some new people sometimes then maybe you won't turn out like your father!" Adelina fires back.

6

Yvette and Mona

~

The massive site on Sanborn is bustling with separate crews and workers, each assigned to different phases of construction; foundation, floor, framework, drywall, siding, the roof, installing electrical wires, and plumbing.

Staying consistent, just as his father had told him, Ronnie hasn't missed a day yet, always bringing twenty-nine sparkling dimes to pay for his taco special. Smartly taking advantage of every available minute with Valerie, Ronnie knows exactly when to take his lunch break from his parents' shop and start heading up the hill on Sanborn to beat the noon rush of hungry construction workers. Valerie's mom is at the customer window. She's at the cash register sorting the bills. Anna notices Ronnie approaching the window.

"Valerie, get up here. Here he comes."

"Coming."

Underneath the leafy eucalyptus trees, little Sunshine is happily playing and carrying on a conversation with her Barbie dolls at the picnic table. Sunshine glances up and spots Ronnie walking up to the lunch truck, "Hi Ronnie!…I'm not supposed to say nuddin' but you're gettin' a surprise today."

Valerie hears her daughter's last words then pokes her head out of the service window, "Sunshine! You little motor mouth! What did I tell you?"

"I didn't say nuddin', Mommy"

Reaching the service window, Ronnie is all smiles. He's never had this much attention paid to him before and he's enjoying every second of it.

As he's been doing for the past several days, Ronnie slowly releases twenty-nine shiny dimes upon the counter. No matter how many times she's seen them before, Valerie's eyes luminate and mouth drops at the very sight of these seemingly glowing coins, "Wow, they're like round diamonds. Can't believe how you get 'em so clean like that, Ronnie."

"I try," Ronnie modestly utters.

"You gotta excuse my daughter. She can be a real blabber mouth sometimes."

"Oh, she didn't say anything."

"Yeah, right. Check you out, trying to protect your little friend."

Valerie looks Ronnie deeply into his eyes then cracks a tiny smile, "Sunshine really likes you Ronnie."

"I like her too," Ronnie nods then asks, "Do you like me, Valerie?"

"Yea, you're different than most of the guys 'round here."

"Different 'cause I'm in the slow class?"

"No, different 'cause you're really nice, Ronnie."

"For real?"

"For real."

Momentarily, Ronnie seems to be mesmerized by Valerie's natural beauty. He's captivated by her perfect eyebrows, her perfect little nose and those perfect succulent lips.

"Are you okay, Ronnie?"

"Uh huh, I like how you don't put on a whole lot of makeup but you're pretty anyway."

"Ahhh, that's so sweet, thank you."

"And you wanna know some'em else, Valerie?"

"What's that?"

"I can't believe you're talking to me."

Valerie blushes as Ronnie struggles to work up enough courage to say the words he was rehearsing over and over last night, "Um, Valerie, um —"

"You wanna ask me some'em, Ronnie?"

"Um, Valerie, would you like to go to a picnic with me?"

"Sure, that'll be nice, Ronnie. Where you wanna go?"

"Oh, sorry. I forgot to say the other stuff."

"Other stuff?"

"Uh huh, see, my parents' gonna come to. They wanna go to Griffith Park. Dad's driving, so we can pick you up."

"Good, I'll bring Sunshine too. She'll like that…It'll be like a double date plus one."

Ronnie's face is shining brighter than the twenty-nines still sparkling on the counter. Valerie reaches underneath the counter and retrieves a small brown bag from a shorten shelf.

"Hey Ronnie, I wanna show you some'em. One of our neighbors on Rowena makes jewelry by hand. His name is Manny an' he's good. That man can make jewelry outta anything."

Valerie slowly empties the contents of the crumbled bag on the counter right next to the small pile of loose shiny dimes. Spilling out of the brown bag are two necklaces made of glowing, connected dimes and two charm bracelets ornamented with shimmering, dangling dimes. One necklace and one charm bracelet are smaller in size.

Ronnie's eyes widen in awe, "Wow.....look at that."

"I get a set and Sunshine gets a set."

Anna is standing a few feet away admiring the happy, gitty-like faces on both her daughter and Ronnie, "Val, go ahead an' put 'em on. Show Ronnie what they look like on you."

While looking directly at Ronnie, Valerie blindly places her necklace around her neck then snaps her bracelet around her wrist as Ronnie stands speechless, completely blown away by the fact that everything in front of him is way better than anything he'd hoped for and envisioned last night.

※※

"Hey Pepe, whatcha need, bro?"

"Yo Pepe, need a driver's license? How 'bout a social security card? Just tell me whatcha need."

"Yo Pepe, I got some good shit for you an' your girl, dude. This shit I got will send you to the fucking moon, dude. Holler at me if ya' want some. I'm right here, Pepe."

"Hey Pepe, you rocked that poetry jam! I'm bringing everybody to hear you at the street fair this year. I can't wait!"

Yeah, this is Echo Park. This is my home turf, and a lot of people 'round here give me my props. Practically everybody 'round here knows me by Pepe. Ever since I grabbed the mike an' started throwing my lyrics out there people 'round here been givin' me big love ever since. I like bringing my girl Teki over here sometimes too so we can chill out here at MacArthur Park. It got its share of piss-stained sidewalks just like everywhere else, but the plush green grass and the spouting water fountain in the center of the manmade lake makes up for all the shady shit going on in and around the park. Sometimes though, MacArthur Park gets a real bad rap. The park maintenance crew considers it a good day when they don't sweep any dead bodies from the bottom of the lake. To be honest though, I've seen more good days than bad days at the park so it's all good wit' me. Matter 'fact, that's where me an' my girl's been at for the past couple hours, just chillin' in the park. We're on our way out now though. Yeah, me an' Teki's gonna kick back an' chill for a minute in my room. It's just a hop away on Figueroa.

I like coming to MacArthur Park though, and I don't mind all the hustlers an' peddlers tryin' to drop their shit on me either 'cause everybody in this fuckin' world gotta hustle. Shit, I don't care if you're sitting behind a big oak desk in a tall ass high-rise an' pulling in six-figures or if you're a sidewalk peddler trying to push a fake Rolex – you're still a hustler. We just give it a different name depending on how we dress an' where we conduct our business, that's all. Teki don't feel as comfortable as I do when we're hanging out here at the park 'cause she says MacArthur brings out my bad side sometimes. Look at this shit, this crazy motherfucker keep staring at Teki.

"Man, I swear to God, Pepe, yo' girl's looking fine as hell…so damn fine, like fine to dine, baby!"

Like I said, I enjoy coming to the park, and I can put up with that hustlers' bullshit, but one thing I absolutely can't stand is a disrespectful motherfucker trying to say shit to my girl an' act like I'm not even there. Matter ' fact, I'm gonna handle this shit right now.

"Yo, motherfucker, whatcha say to –"

"Pepe! Stop! See, that's why I wanted to leave twenty minutes ago. Com'on, Pepe, let's go!" Teki pleads.

Other than the occasional haters an' disrespectful motherfuckers pulling that drama shit, I really like it here. Most of the people here are real to the bone. Since I've been trespassing over to John Marshall, I've noticed how some people living in Silver Lake think that they're better than the people living over here in Echo Park, like they're in some kinda higher class or some shit, but the way I see it, the only difference between Silver Lake and Echo Park is 'em hills – Echo Park ain't got 'em all over the place like that rollercoaster Silver Lake. Another thing I like here is how my mom's place on Figueroa is just a couple blocks from MacArthur Park. That's where we're headed now. I know my girl don't really care too much for my 'hood but being a music lover, her head is always bobbing to that hot Latin rhythm of those catchy Mexican songs blaring out of 'em cheap speakers from all 'em street vendors along the way to Figueroa Street.

"Aw, see, look who's feelin' that cool ass Latin beat...go Teki, go Teki, go Teki, go –"

"Pepe, why don'tcha just shut up an' com'on."

❄❄❄

Pepe and Teki reach 613 Figueroa Street. It's a shoebox bungalow sandwiched between a weathered two-family duplex and a low-rent apartment building. Several kids playing outside briefly stop what they're doing and wave 'hello' to Pepe. In their eyes, Pepe is already a big time player in the business.

"You kids' being good?"

All the kids nod 'yes' then resume playing as Pepe and Teki make their way to the front door. Now, close enough to the door in hearing range, Teki and Pepe simultaneously sigh, "Oh no, not again." From outside, on the front steps, two female voices can be clearly heard inside barking back and forth at one another....

"I'm tired of that bitch always following you around, Mona!"

"Yvette, she have to follow me sometimes 'cause we're picking orders together!"

"Oh yeah? Whatta 'bout that bitch Sonja? She gotta follow you around too?"

"Oh please, Mona, how many times I gotta listen to Miss Wanda say 'Oh Mona, your hair look so pretty today, whatcha do to it to make it so flowy, so flowy…oh please, give me a fuckin' break!"

Outside, Teki is dancing the two-step, trying to contain her bloated bladder.

"Pepe, can we go in now? I gotta pee!"

"Once we hear some'em break then we can go inside. They'll calm down for a minute an' then it'll be safe. I stepped in too early one time an' my head almost got slammed by a flying dinner plate. Com'on, Teki, put yo' ear on the door like this. Listen, it should be coming up any second now," Pepe utters with a knowing nod.

The two heated voices inside are growing louder and louder…

"And why do you keep bringing up stuff from work? I told you before, you shouldn't be bringing work home with you! I'm tired of this shit, Yvette!"

"Fuck you, Mona! You brought it up too!"

"Oh, yeah — well, take this bitch!"

Boom! …Smash!

With one hand holding her crotch and the other wrapped around the door knob, Teki looks at Pepe, awaiting his 'go ahead' nod.

"That's our cue."

"Oh, thank you Jesus!" Teki sighs then bolts inside!

✖❈✖

Inside, Pepe's mom Yvette and her friend Mona are caught off guard. Standing in the living room wearing embarrassed faces, they abruptly get silent and awkwardly straighten their posture as Teki zooms straight across the room then disappears down the hall.

"Hey, Yvette – Mona. Gotta pee! Gotta pee!"

Yvette and Mona could easily be Double Mint twins. Neither one looks a day over thirty-five and their bountiful, sandy blonde hair goes well with their supermodel good looks.

Pepe steps inside and his eyes immediately zero in on the pieces of shattered glass resting in the middle of the floor near the coffee table.

"Mom, why do you two gotta go through this every other day?"

"What? – We was just discussing stuff," Yvette says while glancing at Mona for backup.

"Yea, we was discussing stuff," Mona nods.

The living room walls are covered with framed, poster-size album covers of popular grunge rock bands from the 90's; Alice In Chains, Pearl Jam, Nirvana, Soundgarden, ect.

Pepe can't stand to look at the broken pieces of glass any longer. He bends down and begins to carefully pick up the pieces with his fingers. Pepe gently places the pieces atop the coffee table as Yvette and Mona simultaneously sigh with relief when Teki returns from the bathroom.

"Teki!" Yvette and Mona awkwardly greet in unison.

"Forget it. I'm not rescuing you two. We're supposed to be the kids here. You both need to –"

"Teki!" Yvette pleads.

Eager to liven things up, Mona steps forward, "I know what we can do. Why don't Pepe and Teki ask us some music trivia and then we can forget about this stuff and enjoy the rest of the evening. How 'bout it, guys? You game?"

Teki glances at Pepe with pleading eyes.

"Alright," Pepe sighs.

"Okay, ladies, what was the name of the band that Peter Frampton was in before he went solo?" Teki asks.

Yvette looks at Mona then shrugs her shoulders.

"How about a clue?" Yvette pleads.

"Alright, H – P"

"Hewlett Packard!" Mona quickly blurts out as Pepe and Teki crack a smile.

"Humble Pie," Yvette calmly utters while shaking her head in disbelief at Mona's incredulous response.

"What?" Mona playfully asks.

"Okay, Mom – Mona, what is Bob Dylan's real name?"

"Pepe, that's not fair. Why are you and Teki asking these tough questions?" Yvette asks.

"Mom, you know this one. Okay, okay, here's a hint...Bullshit in Florida."

"Ooo, Ooo, I got it!..Um, Zim..Zimmer...Robert Zimmerman," Mona injects.

"Alright, this should be an easy one for you two. It's a grunge question," Teki nods.

"Yeah, we got this," Yvette winks to Mona.

"Here it is. Where was Eddie Vedder born?"

"That's too easy, Teki. Anybody would know that one," Mona grins.

"For sure, everybody knows that Pearl Jam and Nirvava came out of Seattle," Yvette adds with confidence.

Teki gives the ladies a look then asks, "It's that your final answer?"

Yvette and Mona nod 'yes.'

"Sure, everybody knows that Pearl Jam and Nirvana came out of Seattle, but Eddie Vedder was born in Evanston, Illinois," Teki explains.

"Smart ass," Yvette teases then playfully pokes her tongue at Teki.

"Okay, since you two think you're so smart, what's Eddie Vedder's real name?" Mona asks with a bit of sassiness.

"Edward Louis Severson, the third," Pepe and Teki quickly answers in unison.

"Smart asses," Yvette teases.

"Okay, that's enough. Mom, is there any Cokes in the 'fridge? Me an' Teki's gonna kick it in my room for a minute."

"There's a whole pack. Mona just got some yesterday."

Teki steps away down the hall to Pepe's room as Pepe migrates to the refrigerator and grabs two cans of pop. Yvette and Mona collapse onto the living room sofa then begin to snuggle and find the soft spot of each other's arms.

Some people be looking and staring an' shit when my mom an' Mona be walking together, but me, I don't give a shit. Three years ago, just after I'd turned fourteen and started writing my own shit, Mom said she had some'em serious she wanted to drop on me. It was a Tuesday night, about two minutes to nine. I remember the day and time to the dime 'cause I was all hyped up and ready to watch Def Poetry Hour. Mom almost fucked up my whole night but I cut that shit short real quick. Mom came in my room and sat on my bed next to me looking all serious an' shit. She had that same look you get when there's no food in the house. She told me she started seeing some lady named Mona and they were talking about living together. She wanted to know what I thought about it an' I ran it down quick to her like this, "Mom, my show's gonna start in like a minute so here we go. If I don't care what kinda toothpaste you put in your mouth then why should I care about who you invite between your legs?" Me and Mom had that conversation three years ago. It was over in less than a minute and the subject never came up again. An' that was that.

※⊙※

In contrast to the predominately white grunge rock artists proudly displayed in the living room, Pepe's bedroom walls are covered with colorful posters of prominent black musicians and singers; James Brown, Bob Marley, Curtis Mayfield, Aretha Franklin, Smoky Robinson, Stevie Wonder, Isaac Hayes, ect…

Teki and Pepe are sitting up snuggly close on the bed sipping their Cokes as a mellow soul rhythm fills the air.

"Teki, I need a big favor from you and yo' girls. My dee-jay had to go to Oakland an' he won't be back in time for the Sunset Junction street fair. Can Yello Stuff back me up?"

"I'm sorry, Pepe, but Yello Stuff is a high class professional band. We don't do backups or do low class events," Teki playfully teases then plants a tender kiss on Pepe's cheek, "That's for not bringing up Vince all day, and of course we'll do it. We didn't have anything booked that weekend anyway. Did you finish the lyrics to 'Hear My Echo' yet?"

"I got the bridge down pack but I'm still workin' on a few hooks. I think it's gonna be real sweet once you and the girls bring in that reggae vibe."

"By the way, how'd things go with Kalib? I hope Valerie said no, no, no."

"Matter ' fact, I feel real bad 'cause I didn't even talk to Valerie and –"

"Good, I'm glad. Kalib's got some issues and Valerie don't need to be dealing with somebody like that plus trying to raise a kid too."

"It's worst than that Teki. I'm really worried 'bout Kalib. The shit goin' on at his house ain't no joke. It's some real hard core shit. His mom keeps poundin' on him 'bout his dad an' shit. And I know I'm gonna have to pay in some kinda way for not keepin' my word with Kalib…but when I went to the construction site to holler at Valerie my man Ronnie was already there doin' his thing."

"You can't help yourself, Pepe, you always try to be everybody's friend."

"Yeah, I know…But that shit at Kalib's house though, I swear, that's some serious ass shit. His mom keep poundin' an' poundin' on him about his father…some real heavy shit."

"You know what I think, Pepe, I think Kalib's situation is making you think about your father. You miss your dad, don'tcha?"

"Naw, no way, see those guys up there on the wall?"

"Who? Curtis Mayfield, James Brown, Bob Marley?"

"That's right, they're the ones who raised me, damn straight… taught me all I needed to know 'bout this messed up world."

"Pepe, not to change the subject, but we've been seeing each for a minute now, right?"

"Uh huh"

"Okay, then how come I don't see one single picture of me in your room then?"

Inconspicuously, Pepe purposely spills a dash of pop on his shirt.

"Oh shit, damn!…I'm making a mess like a little kid. Teki, can you get me a clean shirt out of the closet over there?"

"Sure, but you're still gonna answer my question."

Teki opens the closet door and is instantly shocked by the picture in front of her eyes. Behind the closet door is a blown up Yello Stuff promo poster with Teki super imposed in the center. Teki is teary eyed…speechless.

Pepe cracks a smile then teases, "I can't even change my fuckin' clothes without looking at yo' yellow butt."

7
Griffith Park

~

Kalib's mom Adelina has invited the mailman in for a brief chat and morning coffee. The phone rings.

"'Cuse me for a minute while I get that."

"I should be going anyway. Got two more blocks to do. Thanks for the coffee, Adelina."

Adelina waves goodbye while picking up the phone.

"Hello....yes, this is Miss Takesian......Two old cell phones?...... Don'tcha think it would've been more wise to call me before you made the charge to my credit card?........No, no, that's okay, the damage is done now, I'll speak to my son.......thanks, bye."

Adelina marches down the hall. She hears loud Armenian pop music coming from Kalib's bedroom. Adelina twists the doorknob but it's locked. She rapidly knocks on the door.

"Kalib! Kalib! Open the door, I wanna talk to you. And why are you listening to that music this early in the morning?"

"I'm not dressed. Can we talk in an hour?"

"Kalib, why did you need two cell phones?"

"Not new ones, Ma."

"New ones, old ones, who cares, why two, Kalib?"

"Experiment, Ma."

"Experiment? School's closed for summer! Kids don't do experiments during –"

The sudden, loudening Armenian music drowns out Adelina's words. She sighs then walks away.

In her son's bedroom, the loud music is nearly vibrating the walls as a fully dressed Kalib piddles with the delicate, intricate circuitry of the two open cell phones laid out atop a nightstand placed in front of the sofa. Carefully maneuvering a pair of tweezers in between the inner workings of the tiny circuit boards, Kalib intensely studies the cell phones' guts.

❊❂❊

The sky is unusually clear today here in Southern California. A much appreciated Pacific breeze has brushed the thick LA smog out of sight. Ronnie's parents have chosen the perfect day for a picnic at Griffith Park. A stone's throw from Los Feliz, Griffith Park is an excellent getaway for all Angelinos wanting a break from the city's ratrace. Today is special because all park visitors can clearly see the famous, gigantic HOLLYWOOD sign atop Mount Lee. Some people come to this vast park to visit the LA Zoo and the popular gold-domed Griffith Park Observatory where James Dean's bronze bust is fixated on the outside lawn, a tribute to the filming of 'Rebel Without A Cause' at the Observatory in the mid 50's. Other visitors at the enormous park come to enjoy the old-fashioned, scale-down steam trains and a host of other kid-friendly activities such as the pony rides and the colorful merry-go-round.

※❀※

"Valerie, you can't be seen riding in my truck."

Yep, that's what I remember one day three years ago after Rico had got what he wanted from me and I'd asked him after he got off work if we could go to Griffith Park 'cause I'd always heard good things about it from some friends who'd been there, but he flat out told me that he couldn't be seen driving around LA with me in his truck. I was so stupid then. Back then I didn't know exactly what he meant by that and I never asked him either – and now it don't matter anyway.

Three years ago, I learned a lot of stuff the hard way – I know now that I can't ever trust things that come in pretty packages. After my experience with Sunshine's father, I don't know if I could trust a good looking guy ever again. I've seen how ugly guys in pretty packages can be, and compared to Rico, Ronnie's beautiful. I was born in LA and lived my whole life in Silver Lake. I'm seventeen years old now and for the first time in my life I'm going to Griffith Park, a place I'd wanted to go ever since I was a little girl…and it's all happening today because of Ronnie.

When school ended for the summer, I would've never guessed that me and my daughter would be having a picnic in the grass with Ronnie Abelson and his parents. But this is so nice here, sitting on this colorful blanket and enjoying the homemade BLT's Ronnie's mom prepared for us. I don't know how it happened but my little Sunshine is crazy about Ronnie. Just listen to that little motor mouth now as she entertains the Abelsons…

"I really like my necklace an' bracelet. Look, see how they shine an' twinkle in the sunlight. See, my mommy got her's on too. Hers is bigger than mines 'cause I'm small."

Ronald and Amy are grinning cheek to cheek as little Sunshine continues to tell all of her mom's and Ronnie's business...

"See, me an' mom's necklaces an' bracelets was just clean dimes at first. Ronnie would come around lunch time every day and then he started bringing nothing but real clean dimes to pay for his tacos, but I don't think he was hungry though. I think he just wanted to see Mommy and –"

"Alright, alright, that's enough, Sunshine. Let somebody else talk for awhile."

Ronnie high-five little Sunshine then quips, "At least she didn't call you motor mouth."

Valerie sighs then playfully shoots both of them a look.

"Valerie, wanna hear something about Mom and Dad?"

"Sure, Ronnie."

Ronald and Amy glance at one another with crocked smiles, wondering what in the world might come out their son's mouth.

"Valerie, when my dad and my mom was going to school they had to walk up these real high steps after school and Dad used to ask my mom if she wanted him to carry her all the way up the steps and –"

Cutting Ronnie off, his mother giggles then teasingly injects, "Junior, that's true what you're saying about me and Ronald but it sounds like your father left out certain specific details."

"Oh, Lord, help me now," Ronald quips as his wife continues.

"What your father didn't tell you is how he used to lag behind me a few steps on that high staircase, especially on the days I wore a skirt, and he thought I didn't know but he would twist his neck trying to peek up my dress. Junior, don't let your father fool you. He was a gentleman most of the time, but he was a nasty boy all ' the time," Amy nods with an inner, radiant glow of a very happily married woman.

Ronald jokingly hides his face into his open palms as Sunshine, Valerie and Ronnie enjoys a lighthearted chuckle.

Through the corner of her eye, Amy catches Valerie looking at Ronnie in that womanish way…a way that perhaps only another woman understands.

"Honey, why don't you and I take Sunshine for a pony ride," Amy nods to her husband.

"Pony ride! For real? Oh Mommy, can I? Can I, please?" Sunshine excitedly asks.

"Sure, but you better behave yourself an' be a good little girl."

"I promise, Mommy."

The Abelsons take little Sunshine away, leaving Ronnie and Valerie alone on the blanket. Valerie leans over and plants a tender kiss on Ronnie's cheek.

"Ronnie, this is really special. It's my best day ever. Thank you so much."

"I didn't do anything. Mom made the sandwiches and Dad drove the car. I didn't do anything. I just came, that's all."

"You're so silly, Ronnie. You did everything. You made this whole day happen."

"I did?"

While planting another kiss on Ronnie's cheek, Valerie notices a patch of thick bushes and dense underbrush near several trees nearby. She softly whispers, "Wanna go for a little hike, Ronnie?"

"Where?"

"Just over there."

"Okay, let's go."

❊❀❊

Hidden from anyone's view behind a dense wall of underbrush, Valerie leads Ronnie to a brief clearing then slowly lays her body upon the ground. With her right extended upward to Ronnie, she invites him to lie down beside her.

"You ever touched a girl, Ronnie?"

"Like where?"

"You know, down there."

Ronnie shakes his head 'no.' Slowly, Valerie begins to unbutton her jeans then gently grabs Ronnie's left hand and gradually guides his fingers to the tender softness between her thighs.

Certain muscles on Ronnie's face begin to move, muscles he didn't know he had. Muscles in other parts of his body start to come alive as Valerie opens her legs wider to let his fingers enjoy her moist, tantalizing well.

"You like it, Ronnie?"

"Uh huh, feels reeeeeeaal goooood, Valerie."

"Not here, not now, but I got some'em else I wanna give you Ronnie."

"Some'em like a gift?"

"Way better than a gift, Ronnie."

8
The Stairs

~

The name Tip ain't on my birth certificate but it should be. I've been pressing that little button on those spray cans since I was like eight years old. Seems like colors ' been by my side since day one. Other things just come an' go but colors ' always been there for me. It's thicker than blood. I didn't find out half of the shit about my life 'til a few years ago. Some things I still don't know, but what I do know though kinda explains why a box of crayons was more like family to me than anything. When I was a baby my mom just dropped me off one day at my aunt's house and nobody ever heard from her since. My aunt always told me never to call her mommy or auntie in front of anybody 'cause she didn't wanna explain nothing to nobody. She said for me to call her Lisa like everybody else and when she had people over she would tell them that she was just babysitting. One night I was real hungry and couldn't sleep so I got up an' went to the living room where the party was an' I forgot not to say 'auntie' in front of other people an' Lisa back-slapped me so hard I hit the floor, but when I was on the floor I noticed all those bright colors and different shapes in the carpet. Lisa and her friends started laughing at me an' some of 'em thought that I was kinda crazy 'cause instead of me busting out an' crying from Lisa's slap, I just laid there on the carpet and started tracing all the different colored shapes with my fingers, and I told Lisa that the squares, circles, and rectangles looked like people to me. And ever since then, to keep me out of her way, Lisa always made sure I had a box of crayons and paper to draw on. I know Lisa don't like me that much but I'm always gonna respect her though for what she did for me. I'm seventeen now. Me and Lisa still live together but she said that next year, after I graduate from John Marshall, I gotta move out. When me and Brittany started going out, she was the one who got me to open up my first bank account. Brittany taught me to plan for the future, instead of just living day to day. Now, when I get paid from some of my murals I make sure I put some money up in my savings. I never had a girlfriend like Brittany before. She makes me see things in my own paintings that I didn't even notice at first. After she finish up at the TV station later this evening we're gonna meet up and chill for a minute on the stairs tonight.

❊❊

"Tip, you ' been up on that ladder all day. You should come down and get something to eat an' drink. You can get whatever you want from the store – no charge."

That's Mrs. Chang. She's good people. She and her husband owns Descanso Market. They're the coolest bosses I ever had. They're paying me pretty money for this job. This is my first time doing a mural this size. It's huge, and I wanna do my best to make it look good 'cause the Changs deserve that. So far I've been on the ladder scraping the old, peeling paint off the wall and I still gotta ways to go yet before I start putting the base down.

"Thanks, Mrs. Chang, but Brittany's gonna be here soon and I'll be done for the evening. When she comes, I'll bring the ladder in and wash up a little."

"You gotta hot date, huh?"

"Yeah, we're just going to the stairs."

"Ah, the stairs – Mr. Chang got my cherry there one night."

"Mrs. Chang!"

"What? Don't act so innocent, Tip. You know what's happening and I know what's happening too. I maybe sixty-five but I still got it and I'm still here."

"Mrs. Chang, you're just too cool – too cool for me."

"Aw, you – I'm going back in now. Remember ' you're welcome to get whatever you want from the store, any time.

Sometimes I feel so lucky. When I think about my younger years I remember how I used to stay out all night just so I wouldn't be home when Lisa was there – that's when I started tagging for the Silver Lake Boyz – but look at me now. I came a long way, and I definitely ain't never goin' back.

❊❊❊

"Hey you, yeah you, up there on that ladder. You wanna have some fun for fifty dollars?"

"Brittany?"

"Nope, I'm Strawberry."

"Well, Strawberry – Brittany, whoever you are, you're the worst ho I ever seen. The cheapest too. You need to carry yo' butt back to ho school. A ho don't broadcast her asking price upfront like that 'cause the john could be a cop."

"First of all, young man, you need to explain to me how come you know so much about what a ho should or shouldn't be doing and –"

"How'd things go at the station today, Brittany?"

If there's one thing I'd learn about Brittany since we've hooked up it's that she loves to joke an' play around and the best way to break that is to get her talking about the news or anything TV-related. At the drop of a dime, that girl can be cutting up one minute then serious like Oprah the next minute.

"You know, I'm tired of just filing away old digital shows for the archives. That's all I do all day long! The application form said that the chosen intern will be promised a wrap-a-round news spot. You watch, when I go in tomorrow I'm gonna give them a piece of my mind and –"

"Brittany, I'm almost done here – just wanna scrape off a few more inches. There's a lot of old dead skin on this wall."

"Tip, did you listen to anything I was saying or was that one of your tricks to change the subject?"

"Maybe you can talk the station into letting you do a story on a summer intern who doubles at night as a prostitute named Strawberry."

Brittany turns around and quickly scans the ground for any available weapons.

"Ooouch!...Man, that rock hit my leg!"

"Consider yourself lucky 'cause I aimed for your head."

"Hm, and just think, I actually thought I had some high class, ebony princess – but ' come to find out – she's just a cheap, violent ho named Strawberry."

"Tip, get down off‛ that ladder so we can go relax on the stairs. It's been a real hectic day."

"Alright – coming down. I'm gonna take the ladder in and wash up. You wanna come with me an' get some'em from the store. The Changs got my back. Anything from the store is on the house."

"I'm good. Had a late lasagna lunch at the station. I'll just wait here by the wall 'til you get back."

✖✖

Every day Tip tries to distance himself from his past but from time to time it finds its way back…

Waiting for her boyfriend's return, Brittany brushes her long, straighten hair under the dim rays of an old street lamp a few feet from Tip's new concrete canvas. Strolling along the sidewalk with cocky strides that says 'we own this place', four bare-chested thugs branded with loud tattoos, slowly walk up on Brittany.

"Damn, girl, you gotta sweet mama's ass!"

"Yeah, whatcha doin' out here all by ya'self, girl? Ya want us nice gentlemen to walk ya home or some place?"

"Yeah, we'll walk ya home. Huh, fellas?"

"Damn straight, homie."

The brash foursome inch closer to Brittany. Their shifty eyes scan her curves and every inch her smooth, cinnamon skin. Tip turns the corner and discovers his girl encircled by the pack of wolves. Tip notices the signature Silver Lake Boyz tattoo, the bold-stylized 'SLB', imprinted across the back of the necks of his former cohorts.

"Brittany! You okay?"

"I'm okay."

The thugs instantly recognize Tip's voice and quickly turn to face him.

"Tip? You pulled a bad bitch like this?"

"She's not a bitch, she's a lady."

"Lit'l tagger boy done got all proper an' shit – Whatcha think you're better than us now? Well, I tell ya what lit'l tagger boy, every time you start to think you're some'em higher than us you just take a good long look at your fingertip – that spot marked you for life an' you ain't never gonna be nuddin' butta little bitch ass tagger – that fingertip says it all and –"

Suddenly, a powder blue '79 Monte Carlo with tinted windows and 22-inch spinning rims quietly rolls up, seemingly coming out of nowhere. The four thugs immediately step back from Brittany and Tip then straighten their posture. Everybody in Silver Lake knows that car...everyone except for Brittany, as she looks on with a puzzled expression. The passenger side window slowly winds down. Behind a cloud of escaping smoke, a well-known confident voice asks, "Is everything cool, Tip? I hope these fools ain't buggin' you and yo' lady friend."

"Naw, Miguel. Everything's cool. They just came by to see how things was going with my new wall, that's all."

"Alright, Tip...you be cool now."

As the spinning rims of Miguel's Monte Carlo disappear down Descanso, the four gangsters relunctantly give Tip a respectful nod of 'thanks' then quietly walk away down the sidewalk. Brittany stands perplexed. She blurts, "What just happened, Tip? And who was that guy Miguel?"

"Com'on – the stairs."

It's a beautiful night in LA. The air is clean. The sky is clear, as the moon throws its light on the concrete steps climbing upwards to a grassy area where a hilltop house once sat back in the early thirties. It's like this all over Silver Lake. Abandoned staircases stuck on weeded hillsides like harden footprints leftover from Silver Lake's unknown past. During the day, these flight of stairs become a great spot for visiting tourists to snap photographs, and joggers love to utilize the numerous hillside steps peppered around Silver Lake as their perfect exercise routine. During the night, however, when romance fills the air, these isolated concrete staircases become Silver Lake's lovers' lane. Couples come from all over LA to relax and cuddle on these steps while looking up at the stars and talk about their hopes and dreams. Tip and Brittany are midway up on a very popular staircase just a mere block from the Changs' Descanso Market. There are other couples below and above Tip and Brittany, with just the right amount of space in between them for privacy. Brittany is leaning back, comfortably nestled upon Tip's chest. Tip's hands are softly caressing the sides of Brittany's stomach but seems to be slowly traveling upward to the soft rounds of her puffy breasts.

"So, tell me, who was that Miguel guy in that blue car. How'd he know you?"

"Miguel kinda run things in Silver Lake. He came up the hard way an' made it through some real tough shit an' that's why people 'round here give him big props."

"But why did he singled you out back there?"

"It's kinda like a real long story."

"Hey, if you don't wanna tell me, I'm not gonna pressure you. I mean if you –"

"Alright, alright, I get it. Stop the guilt trip…When Miguel's parents got busted for possesion his little brother and sister, Silvia and Juan, was taken to Child Protection right away and then they was going to be placed with a foster family — being that Miguel was too young an' already had a record, he took all the money he'd stashed away and paid this squeaky clean couple pretty money to do this fake foster care thing for him just so he could get them back and raise little Silvia and little Juan himself."

"Wow, that's impressive…But you still didn't answer my question, Tip. Why did Miguel singled you out back at the store?"

"When Miguel got his little brother an' sister from that couple he paid…well, he needed somebody to help him watch Silvia and Juan until he got them better situated with a legit daycare-nanny thing."

"That's so cool that he would do that."

"Dude's gotta big heart."

"Hm, you know, there's nothing said on the news about anything positive that people in the streets might be doing. Hm."

"Not to change the subject but I hope I can finish my new wall before the Sunset Junction street fair starts. It's right around the corner, you know."

"Yeah, I know. And you got plenty of time. But Tip, can I ask you some'em?"

"What's up?"

"Who exactly gave you permission to put your hands all over my chest?"

Baffled, Tip freezes. Amused, Brittany grins.

"I didn't say to stop. I said 'who gave you permission?'"

9
On Air

~

"This is Brittany Steel reporting live from the Steel family home in Silver Lake, California, where last night, a terrible, very terrible injustice took place. When a lot of kids got to stay up to watch 'The Sidewalk Show' on TV at nine o'clock last night, I was cruelly forced against my will to go to bed by two dictators better known around here as Mr. and Mrs. Steel."

Ever since I was ten years old I was making news reports from my very own TV station, which, of course, was the locked bathroom of the Steel family home. Mom's hairbrush was my microphone and the mirror was my audience. And, as usual, just like any other popular reporter or news anchor, not everybody liked what I did so I certainly had my fair share of protesters outside the station. I think I got two little pesty protesters outside my station right now...

"Mama, Brittany's in the bathroom again doing her stupid news report and we gotta brush our teeth!"

"Brittany! Get outta that bathroom right now so your brother an' sister can brush their teeth!"

※❀※

Summer is almost over. Brittany's internship at KRCT has been a real disappointment to her thus far and she's yet to go 'on air.' Since her first day at the station, Brittany has been shadowing and underneath the wings of Laura, KRCT's assistant program director. With three school-age kids at home, Laura has been quietly enjoying her comfortable salary at the station without making any waves for the past eight years. Today though, things will get shaken up a bit at this sleepy little PBS station...

"Good morning, Brittany. I'm running a little behind this morning because I had to drop my daughter off at summer day-camp. It's this new place we're trying out and it's way across town and this LA traffic is just horrendous. Here, grab a donut. It's my turn to bring 'em for the morning meeting. Go' head, grab one. And look at that, I just love your work ethic, Brittany. You took the initiative and filed away the stack of shows I'd left on my desk last night. I really appreciate all –"

"Laura, I know you gotta get to your meeting but can we talk a moment?"

"Sure, Brittany. What's on your mind?"

"Well, it's just that I want to be more useful here but all I've been doing all summer is filing those old digital shows into the archives. The intern application said that I would get a chance to work in the field and –"

"Brittany, you're so right. I'm sorry. Tell ya' what, grab that box of donuts and follow me."

Laura quickly gathers up a few loose papers and a folder from her desk.

"Right now? The meeting?"

"You got it, kid. The meeting. Let's go."

✖✖

A few doors down the corridor from Laura's office is the big conference room where all of the station's programming decisions
are discussed and green-lighted or tossed aside. Carrying the box
of donuts, Brittany is a step behind Laura as they enter the room
centered with a lengthy, glossy-oak conference table seating nine
middle-age men who look more interested in the box of donuts
than anything else.

"Laura, you're late. That's unlike you."

"Long story. Daughter's summer camp, traffic, you get the
picture."

Brittany places the box of donuts on the table next to the coffee pot and the small stack of styrofoam cups. She notices how the
nine men seem to look right through her as if she was some type
of servant…as if she wasn't there at all. They just wanted their
donuts, nothing else. As each man grabbed a donut, Laura nodded
to Brittany to take a seat. To say the least, this gesture raised a few
eyebrows.

"Gentlemen, this is Brittany. I'm sure you all have seen her
going back and forth in the hallways for the past several weeks. She's
our summer intern from John Marshall High School. I'd invited her
to sit in with us at our morning programming meeting, and maybe
she'll learn a thing or two from us old folks, or who knows, maybe
we might possibly learn a thing or two from her."

Laura sighs as she sees that not a single one of her stiff-neck,
button-down comrades had the decency to turn their head towards
Brittany to nod a 'welcome' or say 'hello' to her, but yet, five of the
men didn't waste any time peeping into the box of donuts, hoping
for seconds.

"Laura, aren't you having your usual coffee and donut this morning?", one of the stuffy suits asks.

"No, not this morning. For some reason I've lost my appetite," Laura sighs with a touch of sarcasm.

Laura wants to get things started. She scans the notes in her folder.

"Looking at the schedule here it looks like we're set through next Wednesday. How are we looking for next Thursday's local spot? Anybody got anything?"

As Brittany's hand slowly rises, each of the nine men begin to shake their heads in frustration at her mere presence. Laura happily nods to Brittany, gesturing her to speak.

"How about a series called 'Silver Lake's Unsung Heroes'?

Brittany's idea ignites a spark in one of the suits, "Beatrice, that's a terrific idea! I betcha Silver Lake has quite a few military veterans living here."

"Sir, my name's not Beatrice. It's Brittany and —"

"Young lady, whatever your name is, I'm with you on this and —"

"Well, maybe I should've been more clear. I'm not talking about unsung heroes like war veterans. And please don't misunderstand me. I have an uncle serving over in Afghanistan right now as we speak. He's in the Marines, so trust me when I say that I have nothing but respect for our soldiers, but you gotta admit though, there's definitely not a shortage of news coverage about them anywhere. But do we ever hear anything positive about gang members?"

All eyes turn towards Laura. The men look rattled. Laura smiles, seemingly enjoying every second of this meeting now. One of the suits slams his fists atop the table!

"Laura, what is this? She's talking about gangs! This is a PBS station!"

Brittany spring up with fire in her eyes. She defiantly defends herself and makes her point, "Look, I know that being a PBS station there should be an educational angle to every story we do, and there will be. I think it's about time we explore and spotlight the positive people of Silver Lake who wouldn't ordinarily get recognized. And we wouldn't be glorifying gangs or the gang lifestyle but just focusing on some of the positive things that some of these people are doing out in the community and we don't even know about it 'cause we won't even look at them or even talk to them!"

"But, young lady, keep in mind that you're talking about gang members and that will bring the criminal element into the story, and I just don't know if our regular audience will put up with that and —"

"Look, I've seen some of the local stories KRCT have done and just how many times do your audience have to watch another story about some tree root breaking ground and tearing up the sidewalks? Just tell me when was the last time KRCT took a reporter and a camera into, not just Silver Lake, but into Echo Park, Chinatown, Boyle Heights or Crenshaw and maybe interviewed a panhandler or a homeless person? Or isn't that educational enough for you?" Brittany snarls as the men's eyes begin to stare her up and down like an unwanted delinquent.

The cold stares are too overwhelming for young Brittany. She storms out of the room, full of tears...her spirit crushed. Around the table, mumbled whispering spreads...

"Who does she think she is anyway?"

"Can you believe that?"

"What nerve…unbelievable."

Laura shakes her head in disgust at the whispering and soft chatter from the men.

"Okay, that's enough! I've heard enough already! Just listen to you guys…..Listen, that young girl was me years ago. That young girl was you years ago, full of fire and full of heart! But just look at us now. What happened to us? Did we lose it?….I say we bring Brittany back in here and let her bring our dead asses back to life!"

There's an awkward moment of silence, then slowly, each of the suits begin to turn to the one seated next to him. Simultaneously, they all burst with chuckles and hearty laughter!

"Dead asses! Ha ha ha!"

"Dead ass?…What a beauty, I tell ya!"

"I haven't been called a dead ass in years! Ha ha ha!"

"Dead ass? Ha ha ha…I think my ol' army drill sargeant back in boot camp used to call us that! Ha ha ha"

"You sure that wasn't your wife who called you that? Ha ha ha"

As the laughter fades, one of suits' faces turn serious.

"Laura, you're right. How about we break her in gradually? We got the Silver Lake Sunset Junction coming up. Maybe we can do some in-house training then send her out to the street fair with a small camera crew. If she does well at the fair then we can let her try out some of her new ideas."

Laura stands and heads toward the door.

"I better see if I can catch her before she leaves the building. I'll be right back."

As Laura turns the knob and opens the door, a bright-eyed, grinning Brittany stands with open arms and softly nods, "I knew you had my back."

10

Rowena Avenue

~

Kalib is marching up Sanborn with that focused determination that usually scares people away. It's this very tunnel vision of his that will decide his fate. Right now, Kalib has just one wish, and he's anxious to find out if it'll be realized. No matter how many times Valerie has turned him down, Kalib has this wild notion that somehow she will one day give in and go out with him. There's a hundred thoughts racing through Kalib's head right now as he gets closer to the bustling construction site. There's that faraway, thousand mile stare in Kalib's eyes that he sometimes get as he makes his way up the hill. He thinks to himself, 'This is my one last chance. If Valerie says yes to hanging out with me at the Sunset Junction street fair then everything will be alright. Nobody will get hurt. It's my last hope to make this a good summer after all. I hope she says yes.'

Kalib reach the driveway leading into the vast construction site. Standing beside a beefy Dodge Ram pickup, Kalib looks over towards the corner where the lofty eucalyptus trees throw shade over the picnic tables and Valerie's mom lunch truck. Instantly, Kalib freezes as his whole world seems to shatter right before his eyes. This is certainly not the way things suppose to be today. Leaning out of the service window, Valerie twirls her fingers around her charmed necklace while easing romantically close to Ronnie's face. Kalib stomps his foot then angrily slams his forearm against the side of the pickup, "Fuck!"

※※

Later that evening, the sun slowly fades as Ronnie steps along Rowena Avenue, a seemingly quiet street lined with tall, wind-mill palm trees. Carrying three long-stem, red roses in his left hand, Ronnie constantly looks side to side at every house. It's obvious that he's never walked along this section of Rowena before. Down the street, a tan, tinted-window lowrider makes an abrupt U-turn then slowly eases back towards Ronnie. The lowrider makes wild turns in the middle of the street as if there were no rules, or the driver lives by his own rules. Nonchalantly, Ronnie continues his journey as if the spoke-rimmed Buick Regal slowly following him wasn't there at all. Simultaneously, all tinted windows begin to roll down, releasing the thomping beat of an old school jam.

"Hey, turn that shit down while I holler at this fool."

The music dies as the driver slightly pokes his tattooed neck out to speak to Ronnie.

"Yo, home, where ' you from?"

Politely, Ronnie stops and turns to answer the question.

"I live in Silver Lake, California."

"Dude, I know that — Who ' you run with?"

"I don't run. I walk. Who ' you run with?"

"S — L — B......all the way, homie."

There's a few chuckles coming from the three tatted thugs sitting laidback on the passenger side and in the backseat.

"Man, let's cruise. That fool's crazy."

"Yo, leave the dude alone, man. He's on the slow train, you know."

"Alright, home, we're gonna cruise, but can I ask you some'em?"

Ronnie cordially nods, "Uh huh."

"Who's the flowers for?"

"Valerie, Sunshine and Anna."

"Valerie? Valerie down the street? Anna's Valerie?"

"Yep"

"Damn!....Everybody's been trying to tap that! How'd you do that? What's yo' secret, player?"

Ronnie ponders a second then nods with a mile-long smile, "Twenty-nine dimes."

"I don't know what the fuck ya talkin' about, home, but if it works, it works."

"It worked," Ronnie nods as the tan lowrider pulls away.

❇❇

Minutes later, Ronnie sees the lunch truck he's visited a thousand times parked in the driveway at 6103 Rowena Avenue. With the three roses in tow, Ronnie rings the doorbell. Looking sizzling hot, Valerie answers the door wearing skin-tight, blue jean shorts and a revealing low-cut top.

"Hey, Ronnie. Told ya I'm just a short walk from you. Whatcha got there?"

"Just some roses. This one is for you. This one's for your mom, and this one is for Sunshine."

Teasingly, Valerie gives Ronnie a scornful look.

"You mean to tell me that you came to my house with roses for two other women?"

Ronnie is having a hard time digesting Valerie's comment. He stands awkwardly frozen, trying to figure out if she was serious or not.

"I'm sorry, Valerie. Did I do something wrong?"

"No, it was a joke, Ronnie. Com'on in. My mom's at bingo and I think Sunshine probably fell asleep already. She tired herself out playing outside this evening. I'll find a vase and put these in some fresh water. Come in."

Ronnie steps inside. He looks anxious. He wants to ask Valerie something but is having trouble bringing it up. Valerie hurries into the kitchen. She finds a tall glass and places the roses inside then fills it with cold water. She turns around and notices Ronnie standing in the living room with a twisted face.

"Ronnie, is everything okay?"

"Um, I know you said we're going to watch a movie first, but if Sunshine's not —"

"Oh my God, what is it with you two?.....Alright, com'on, you can take a peek at that little motor mouth but if she's asleep and wakes up then this date is over."

Innocently, Ronnie smiles in anticipation of seeing little Sunshine. Teasingly, Valerie shoots Ronnie a look for ignoring her half-hearted ultimatum. It's a short walk to the left hallway. They reach Sunshine's bedroom door. Quietly, Valerie opens the door. A night light softly illuminates the colorful room. Ronnie's smile grows wider as he watches Sunshine quietly sleep. Valerie leans closer to Ronnie's ear then whispers, "You know what I like the most when she's sleeping? I like it when that little mouth of hers shuts down for eight hours."

Once again, Valerie fires another look at Ronnie as she gets no response whatsoever to her playful comment. Then it hits her, truly sinks in. It's at this very moment in which Valerie realizes that Ronnie cares just as much for her daughter as he does for her. She gestures Ronnie to step inside to get a closer look at Sunshine. Happily, Ronnie eases next to Sunshine's bedside. He notices the necklace holder perched atop the nightstand displaying her Barbie's jewelry and her beloved dime-charmed bracelet and necklace. Thinking that Ronnie could stand there for hours, Valerie intervenes. She quietly walks in, hooks Ronnie's arm and gently pulls him out into the hallway.

❊❊

Sharing a large bowl of popcorn, Valerie is snuggled close to Ronnie on the living room couch. The credits begin to roll on the TV screen.

"You liked the movie?"

"I liked the movie and the popcorn too. I like it here."

Ronnie looks around the room at the framed pictures and fancy art pieces mounted on the walls then something steals his attention. It's a two-foot, encased, silver trophy proudly displayed atop its own table in the left corner.

"Is that your trophy, Valerie?"

"Nope, that my mom's. She's so proud of that thing. She won first prize at the street fair last year for best mobile food vendor. And she swears up and down that she's gonna win it again this year."

"I'll vote for her any day. Anna's tacos' the best."

"Hey, before I forget, I wrote a little something for you, Ronnie."

"I didn't know you liked to write."

"Yeah, I kinda keep it to myself."

"Was that the gift you was talking about at the park?"

Valerie points to her bedroom down the other hallway then softly whispers, "No, that's in there. You can open it after you hear my poem."

"A poem? What's it called?"

Fishing a folded sheet of paper from the back pocket of her jean shorts, Valerie teases, "Now you better not laugh. It's called 'Ronnie.'"

"I like it so far," Ronnie nods.

"Ready to hear it?"

"Uh huh"

Too embarrassed to look at Ronnie's reaction, Valerie holds the sheet of paper in front of her face then begins to cite her poem...

> "Summer.
> Dimes.
> Love.
> Ronnie."

There's a moment of silence. Valerie slowly peeks around the corner of the paper.

"So, whatcha think?"

"Oh, it's over? I thought you was just warming up, you know, practicing."

"Never mind," Valerie sighs.

"No, don't get sad 'cause I really liked it. That's really cool how you did that in just four words. It's kinda like a game, huh?"

"Yeah, I guess you can call it a game, a kinda poetry game. Go 'head, you try it."

"Naw, I'm not good at stuff like that."

"Aw, com'on, Ronnie. Anybody can do it. It's easy........Okay, I'll help you. Let's try this. Just look at me and say the first four words that you think about. You ready?"

Ronnie scoots closer to Valerie. He slowly raises his right hand and let his fingers travel gently across her succulent lips. Four words begin to flow from his mouth...

"Beautiful.

Valerie.

Perfect.

Valerie."

Valerie blushes.

"I kinda cheated 'cause I used your name two times."

Valerie plants a juicy kiss on his lips then whispers, "You can cheat and use my name any time you want, Ronnie."

"Oooo, that feels good. Can you do it again? Your lips are so soft, Valerie."

"I gotta better idea. Let's go in my bedroom. I think it's time for you to open your present now."

Valerie stands and leads Ronnie out of the living room.

❄❄

Ronnie follows Valerie into her dimly lit bedroom. Immediately, Ronnie's eyes fall upon the tree-like necklace holder fixed atop the nightstand next to Valerie's elegant canopy bed covered with flowery drapes. Ronnie nods pleasingly at the sparkling dime-charmed bracelet and necklace dangling from the jewelry tree. Valerie climbs upon her bed underneath the colorful awning, then, without words, she turns and gives Ronnie a look he's never seen before. It's a very inviting, tantalizing look. Methodically, piece by piece, almost in slow motion, Valerie begins to peel off her blue jean shorts...her low cut top...her pink panties...her pink bra.

11
The Street Fair

~

It's Friday, a day before the start of Silver Lake's highly-anticipated, two-day Sunset Junction street festival. Tip's been up all night putting the finishing touches on his latest creation for the Changs' Descanso Market. In celebration of the mural's completion, the Changs are hosting a cookout for Tip and his closest friends. With the Changs' blessing, Tip couldn't think of a better way to show Silver Lake's community spirit in the mural — as the Changs had requested — than to have his own circle of diversified friends featured on the concrete canvas. The thirty-foot, colorful wall depicts Teki, Brittany, Pepe, Valerie holding little Sunshine's hand, Ronnie, Kalib, and Tip shopping between two well-stocked aisles as Mr. and Mrs. Chang stand cheerfully near the checkout counter with a vibrant sign hanging above that reads...

WELCOME TO THE DESCANSO MARKET

IT'S EVERYBODY'S STORE!

Mr. Chang is outside turning over the burgers and hot dogs behind a smoky grill as Tip, Brittany, Teki, Pepe, Valerie and Ronnie take turns standing next to the vibrant wall while someone snaps a quick photo. Tip looks around then steps into the street to see if anyone's walking up the sidewalk.

"Anybody seen Kalib?"

"I called his house yesterday and his mom said that she would remind him to come."

Inside the store, Mrs. Chang is going over a few details and responsibilities for nine-year-old David and his brother, eleven-year-old Roberto. About three weeks ago, Mr. Chang caught the two boys stealing five Snickers and four BabeRuth candy bars. As they've been doing for years, the Changs never call the cops on the little kids who shoplift, but instead, conduct their own punishment system. The hard labor sentence handed down to David and Roberto was for them to come to the store twice a week for the rest of the summer to do clean up chores. The Changs wanted the boys at the store today to help keep an eye on things while they celebrate Tip's mural. David and Roberto are standing up straight and giving Mrs. Chang their undivided attention as she run things down, "Now, see the brooms over there in that corner? You each grab a broom and sweep the aisles, and if a customer comes then one of you come outside and let me or Mr. Chang know while the other one stay inside. You boys got any questions before I go outside?"

"No ma'am," Roberto politely shakes his head.

On the other hand, little David has something he's been itching to ask, "Um, Mrs. Chang, after we get finish sweeping in here, um, can we get a hamburger from the grill?"

"First you steal our candy and then you want us to give you a hamburger?"

Little David is embarrassed. He looks down at his dirty sneakers, avoiding any eye contact with Mrs. Chang.

Mrs. Chang steps away. When she reach the door she abruptly turns around and looks little David squarely in the eye then nods with a gleeful grin, "How about two big double cheeseburgers for my two best workers."

"Alright!"

"That's what I'm talkin' about!"

Elated, the boys race to the corner to grab the brooms!

※❈

It's Saturday, the first day of the annual street festival. In the heart of Silver Lake, where the main arteries meet, the paved pathways are blocked off and filled with several stages for the numerous bands and spoken word artists scheduled to appear, carnival rides, ice cream and mobile food vendors, balloon clowns and other street performers, local painters, tattoo artists, palm readers, jewelry makers and other handmade crafters. For one weekend, at the end of summer, Silver Lake throws a big party and shows off its talented, gifted artists. For two days, people from all over LA and Southern California track to Silver Lake, giving local artists like Tip, Pepe and Teki's band Yello Stuff the kind of exposure that could possibly get them to an even higher level.

This is the day Valerie's mom has been waiting for all year long. The opening day of the festival includes the mobile food vendors competition and Anna's Taco Box has some tough competition this year. Lined up, side by side, the colorful lunch trucks all have catchy names such as Sushi Heaven, Hot Dogs On Wheels, Burgers To Love, Fish Out Of Water, ect...

The twelve official food-tasting judges are now putting on their distinctive orange 'food judge' T-shirts as each food each are preparing their best sample dish. Across the street, on the other side of a steady flow of pedestrians, Ronnie and his parents are treating little Sunshine to a cone of soft-serve ice cream. Valerie is helping her mom prep their tacos for the judges and she spots her daughter standing with Ronnie and the Abelsons near the ice cream stand.

"Ronnie, don't let her eat so much ice cream!" Valerie yells.

Apparently, the amplified rock music from a nearby band stand along with the crowd chatter have drowned out Valerie's words. Taking a big lick of her ice cream, little Sunshine happily waves to her mom across the path of pedestrians as Valerie shakes her head and sighs. Seemingly, out of thin air, Kalib suddenly appears right in front of Valerie. He's standing at the service window as Anna hastily garnishes the sample platter that will hold her award-winning tacos. Anna shoots Valerie a look, gesturing her to get rid of Kalib.

"Hi, Valerie, how are —"

"Kalib, this is a bad time, we're about to —"

Nothing Valerie is saying seems to be registering to Kalib. He seems more interested in Anna's lunch truck than anything else. Inconspicuously, his shifty eyes are measuring every inch of the chrome-trimmed truck. Valerie senses that he's not going away. She sighs then puts on a cordial face.

"Where were you yesterday, Kalib? Did you see Tip's new mural? It's really cool. You gotta see it."

Kalib's mind is elsewhere, far from Silver Lake and definitely far from any concerns with Tip's new wall. He asks, "Valerie, do you think I'm a good person?"

"Sure you are, Kalib. You're smart and everybody knows that you like computers and stuff like that," Valerie seems to be running out of words then awkwardly repeats herself, "Sure, you're a good guy and –"

"Valerie, would you like to walk around a little with me and maybe we can get some ice cream and –"

Valerie notices the team of orange-shirted food judges nearing their taco truck.

"The judges are coming. My mom needs me here right now. I'm sorry, Kalib."

"I understand. Goodbye, Valerie."

Valerie's face turns puzzled as Kalib does an about face and disappears as quietly and quickly as he'd appeared a few minutes ago. The strange peculiar way Kalib uttered 'goodbye' like that, in such a blunt, hard way is making Valerie wonder about him, "Hm."

12
Hear My Echo!

~

Surrounded by a small camera crew, Brittany positions herself a few steps away from the heavy pedestrian traffic as she gives her live report, "As you can see all around me, thousands have come out on this gorgeous Southern California day to the second and final day of this annual street festival here in Silver Lake. One of the special events being presented today, on stage six I'm told, will be the highly popular spoken word competition and we'll be sure to bring you a live report on that event later at two o'clock. This is Brittany Steel reporting for KRCT, coming to you live from Silver Lake's Sunset Junction street fair, back to you at the station Joyce."

❈❈

A sizeable crowd have gathered around stage six. Pepe and Teki's all-girl band Yello Stuff are on the platform testing the microphones and amplifiers. After a quick check, Teki fine-tunes her guitar strings as the other girls nod to her, signaling that they're set and ready to play. Teki is dressed in her trademark look; half-dyed purple hair with a few strands streaking down on one side underneath a yellow bandana. Teki nods to Pepe as the girls begin to play a soft reggae rhythm. Pepe steps up to the edge of the stage. He brings his mike up to his lips and greets the enormous crowd, "Hey now, hey! What's up! They call me Pepe and these beautiful young ladies behind me pumping out that cool rhythm is..... Yello Stuff! Let's hear it for the ladies, y'all!"

The crowd comes alive and erupts with applause.

Rocking to the smooth, steady beat, Pepe continues, "First of all, I wanna thank Yello Stuff for filling in for me, especially on such short notice. Man, I tell ya, I love that reggae flavor!.....And I wanna thank the Sunset Junction committee for inviting me to perform once again here at this year's Silver Lake Spoken Word Competition....Yeah, y'all hear that smooth reggae groove? Yeah, y'all like that, don'tcha?"

The crowd responds with thunderous applause.

"Let's hear it again for Yello Stuff, y'all!"

The crowd explodes with whistling cat calls and loud cheers.

"Y'all, this is a lit'l some'em I wrote called 'Hear My Echo!' It's not necessarily all about that fucked up shit that went down in Florida but it is what it is....Y'all ready?"

The crowd roars with another round of explosive cheers.

Pepe coolly nods to Teki three times then starts to rap as Teki and the girls continue to play a rhythmic reggae beat, totally in sync with Pepe's lyrical flow...

"Yeah I'm mad an' I'm way too young.

I don't like standing in Florida – facing a courthouse gun.

Peep into my world and you twirl n' swirl.

Can't handle what yo' eyes might see.

Ain't no fuckin' way you wanna be me.

Walkin' in my shoes.

Be ready to pay some dues.

Yeah hear my echo!

I wanna scream!

Why is this fuckin' world so got damn mean?

I don't like this shit happening all around me.

Motherfuckers killin' people an' getting' off scott free!

They're making me angry and angry and angrier!

Go ahead 'cause I'm just gonna get louder and louder!

They try to tell me what to say and teach me what they know.

I'm tired of their shit and tired of their pony show!

Com'on now Silver Lake!...Hear my echo!"

❋❋❋

Just as Valerie's mom had wished, Anna's Taco Box is once again the first-place prize winner of this year's mobile food vendors contest. Wrapped with the winner's blue ribbon, the shiny silver trophy is proudly displayed on Anna's service counter. Valerie is at the window handing a customer his tacos. Looking up, Valerie notices her daughter's father Rico walking hand-in-hand with a very attractive young lady near the ice cream stand. The young lady gets a cone but Rico doesn't. Rico plants a quick kiss upon her cheek then migrates through the moving pedestrian traffic towards Anna's taco truck. Valerie sighs as Rico steps up to the service window. Rico notices Anna standing a short distance next to Valerie. From the disapproving expressions, Rico knows that he's not welcomed here but there's something important he must discuss with Valerie. In his futile attempt to break the ice with Anna and Valerie, Rico utters, "Congratulations on taking first place, Anna. Nobody can beat your tacos. And Valerie, that's a nice necklace you're wearing. I never seen one made out of dimes before."

Anna steps in front of Valerie with a tighten face, "Rico, I'm sorry but we don't serve pigs here."

"Alright, alright. Look, I didn't come over here to argue with nobody. Valerie, can I talk to you for a minute?"

Valerie glances at her mom. Biting her lips, Anna steps away.

Before Rico has a chance to speak, Valerie takes a quick jab at him, "So Rico, I saw that girl you was with. She's pretty. Do you let her ride in your truck?"

Rico shakes his head in frustration then spits, "Damn it, Valerie. That girl you're talking about over there is my wife! That's why I've been trying to call you so many times but you never answered. You see, I told my wife about our daughter and she said that she would like to get to know her and maybe she could come visit with us sometimes, maybe stay on the weekends."

Eavesdropping, Anna has heard enough. She can't restrain her thoughts any longer, "I told ya! We don't serve pigs here!"

Rico doesn't make eye contact with Anna. He totally ignores her but Valerie hits him just as hard as her mom, "So now you wanna spend time with your daughter, huh? Rico, can you even tell me your daughter's name?"

Rico stands speechless. Valerie gives him a look then glances through the moving crowd and notices Ronnie and her daughter standing in line at the popular ice cream stand. With her sparkling necklace and charmed bracelet glistening in the bright California sun, little Sunshine catches her mom's eye then waves hello. Brittany and her skeletal camera crew are a short distance away, randomly picking passing pedestrians out of the crowd for a quick, impromptu interview. Unbeknownst to Brittany, Kalib turns the corner a few yards away then heads straight towards her, as if he's drawn to the camera like a magnet. Oddly, Kalib is carrying a black plastic bag, the kind of dark bag a customer gets when buying a large bottle of beer from a convenience store. Caught off guard, Brittany is now awkwardly face to face with Kalib who seems to be anxiously desiring some air time. Brittany's small crew shrugs their shoulders and gesture her to roll with it. Brittany sighs then nods to Kalib, "So, tell me, are you enjoying the street fair?"

Looking dead into the camera, Kalib puts on his harden soldier's face and begins to shout, "Never forget! They killed my people but I'll never forget! Armenian genocide happened and I'll never forget!"

Taken completely by surprise, Brittany and her crew silently mouth, "What the fuck!" Then, as if she's been training for a moment like this all of her life, Brittany's natural reporter instincts automatically seems to kick in. Holding her professional composure, Brittany looks straight into the camera and skillfully saves the piece, "As you can see, folks, the Sunset Junction street fair is as eclectic as the Silver Lake community itself. There's something for everybody here, regardless of your race or ethnicity, so com'on down and catch the final hours of this wonderful, festive event."

Impressed and pleased with Brittany's quick-thinking reporter skills, her camera crew nods and gives her a well-deserving thumbs up. Kalib disappears without a single word to anyone. Around the corner, Rico is persistently trying to persuade Valerie to let his daughter start regular visits with him and his wife. Anna is getting fed up with Rico's presence as a lady gives her order while looking over Rico's shoulder.

"Can't you see you're blocking our customers!" Anna scorns.

The line at the ice cream stand is stretched pretty long. Sunshine gets fidgety and begins to look around. Something peculiar catches her attention. She notices a man carrying a black bag walking speedily towards her grandmother's taco truck. Suddenly, Kalib appears behind the lady and Rico, then inconspicuously, he places the black plastic bag atop the corner of the counter then quickly walks away. Little Sunshine breaks out of the ice cream line to alert the young man about his bag. Ronnie is unaware of Sunshine taking off.

"Hey! Yo' bag! You forgot yo' bag!"

Kalib turns around with his cell phone held tightly in the palm of his right hand. He aims the phone directly at the black bag now resting on Anna's counter.

"Yo' bag!" Little Sunshine points.

"Fuck! Little girl, get out of the way! Move!" Kalib yells!

Ronnie recognizes Kalib's voice then realizes that Sunshine is not by his side. Frantically, Ronnie looks around for her.

The yelling reaches Rico's ears. He peeks closely at the black bag just mere inches to the left of him and notices the tiny antenna protruding out of the top.

"What the fuck is this?" Rico alarms while turning around.

It's too late. Kalib punches a few numbers on his cell phone and the thunderous blast sends Anna's truck ten feet into the air! People standing safely away are rubbing the painful echo of the resounding blast from their ears as they shake their heads in utter disbelief.

"What's going on?"

"Oh my God!"

"Jesus Christ!"

"Oh Lord, help us!"

"He did it! Security! Security! He did it! Security!"

Blood-stained debris and severed body parts splatter across the ground. Kalib hastily turns then vanishes. Protruding from underneath Anna's overturned taco truck, Rico's bloody legs make their last twitch.

❄❄

Nearing his house at 192 Prospect Avenue, Kalib slows his jog. Sunday is his mother's house cleaning day. Adelina is busy vacuuming the living room carpet as Kalib steps inside. Puzzled, she glances at the wall clock then turns off the vacuum cleaner.

"I thought you was going to the street festival. Why are you sweating like that? Are you okay, Kalib?"

At the moment, Kalib and Adelina are in two separate worlds. Absolutely nothing she is asking or saying to him is getting through. The only thing on Kalib's mind right now is figuring out a way to get his mother out of the house. Then, it hits him. Her flowers.

"Mom, when I came in I noticed that maybe those rabbits again ' been eating at your flowers outside. They're all messed up, stems broken off and leaves all on the ground like crazy."

"Oh, no, not again," Adelina sighs while pushing the vacuum cleaner aside then stepping towards the front door.

Satisfied, Kalib marches straight down the hall to his bedroom. Adelina opens the door and stands frozen in shock as a barricade of police cruisers and countless rifle barrels are pointed straight at her head.

"My Lord…What in the world," Adelina sighs in disbelief.

Inside, Kalib calmly points his cell phone at the black plastic bag placed slightly behind the lamp atop his nightstand.

Outside, a loud voice projected from a cop's megaphone warns Adelina, "Ma'am, put your hands up and —"

The enormous blast knocks Adelina to the ground as shattered glass burst through every window!

❀❀❀

At the street fair, Ronnie's stiffen, blood-stained body is humped over on the ground as little Sunshine, crying hysterically for her mother, crawls from underneath his lifeless arms,

"Mommy? Mommy?"

Knocked unconscious and thrown to the bottom corner of their overturned truck, Anna and Valerie slowly comes to and then tries to rub away the throbbing pain from the side of their heads. Valerie struggles to stand then frantically calls out for her daughter, "Sunshine? Sunshine? My baby? Sunshine?"

❀❀❀

Another school year begins at John Marshall High...

So we're seniors now. Most of us made it through the summer. Our circle on the quad won't be the same. Kalib never did got used to calling me Pepe. Guess he ain't gotta worry 'bout that now. I still feel terrible about not telling him early on that Valerie and Ronnie had something going on – maybe if I'd told him early enough then maybe he and Ronnie would still be here. It's times like now when I miss talking to Miss Kelley. She always knew exactly what to say to help me get through tough shit like this. I don't know where she's at now, but I really miss her. I wish all my teachers was like Miss Kelley. I wonder how she's doing?

Epilogue

~

Two thousand miles away in Mayville, Kansas, thirty high school students are sluggishly entering a classroom. The teacher writes in the upper left corner of the blackboard the class subject and her name underneath...

Language Arts
Miss Kelley

As the students drag their feet and continue to shuffle in, Miss Kelley writes a message in the center of the blackboard in bold, chalky letters...

JUST LET IT OUT!

A Personal Message from the Author

~

I am aware that the Silver Lake Sunset Junction Street Fair has been discontinued due to permit fee issues, but I hope that readers of this book will rejuvenate and spark a renewed interest and make concrete efforts to bring back the street fair not only in Silver Lake, but in other communities as well.

Also, my heart goes out to the Armenian people, especially to those Armenian families who have suffered and sacrificed gravely at the cruel hands of the Turks during the 1915 – 1923 Armenian Genocide period.

Lastly, when I ran in the Los Angeles Marathons (two years in a row) and noticed the eclectic, diverse neighborhoods along the 26-mile marathon route, I knew then that one day I would have to write a story with the city itself as a central character. So, finally, here it is…'29 Dimes : A Love Story'.   – Randolph Randy Camp

Acknowledgement

1. Song lyrics to 'VEHICLES', as sung by the character Teki, and the spoken word lyrics to 'HEAR MY ECHO!', as performed by the character Pepe, were written and copyrighted by the author Randolph Randy Camp.

2. The detailed description of the three murals, 'FLOWERS', 'TEARDROPS', and 'EVERYBODY'S STORE', as painted by the character Tip, were conceived and originated by the author Randolph Randy Camp.

Other Novels By
Randolph Randy Camp

~

About the Author

~

Randolph Randy Camp was born on March 12, 1961 in rural Spotsylvania County, Virginia. Randy is a Quarter-Finals Winner of the prestigious Writers Network Annual Screenplay and Fiction Competition. Randy has five daughters, Natasha, Melinda, Randie, Christina, Ranielle, and one son Joshua. Two of Randy's all-time favorite quotes are 'Don't let others define you – You define yourself!' and 'Don't be afraid to dream BIG!'

For More Info about author Randolph Randy Camp, please visit https://www.amazon.com/author/randolphcamp or http://randy0312.wordpress.com

CPSIA information can be obtained at www.ICGtesting.com
Printed in the USA
BVOW04s2058050115

382035BV00005B/25/P